ELLIE'S WAR
Come Home Soon

EMILY SHARRATT

■ SCHOLASTIC

Scholastic Children's Books
An imprint of Scholastic Ltd
Euston House, 24 Eversholt Street, London, NW1 1DB, UK
Registered office: Westfield Road, Southam, Warwickshire, CV47 0RA
SCHOLASTIC and associated logos are trademarks and/or
registered trademarks of Scholastic Inc.

First published in the UK by Scholastic Ltd, 2014

Text copyright © Scholastic Ltd, 2014

ISBN 978 1407 14494 8

Printed by CPI Group (UK) Ltd, Croydon, CR0 4YY
Papers used by Scholastic Children's Books are made
from wood grown in sustainable forests.

1 3 5 7 9 10 8 6 4 2

www.scholastic.co.uk

*With special thanks
to Emma Young*

One

Ellie felt the plate slipping from her wet fingers and watched it bounce off the tiled floor and shatter into four jagged pieces. She froze for a moment, her eyes fixed on one of the china shards as it finally came to rest, glistening prettily against the dark-coloured floor.

Ellie unstuck her tongue from the roof of her mouth with an audible *tuck* and, at last, raised her eyes to her mother, who had been standing in the doorway.

"I'm sorry, Mother," she began hastily, but she could see it was too late. Her mother's scowl was deepening by the second. Her cheeks were flushed dark red as though she'd been slapped.

"Did you do that deliberately?"

"No, of course n—"

"Josephine," Aunt Frances piped up from the table, her blue eyes wide, "it was clearly an accident."

Ellie closed her eyes. She loved her aunt very much but speaking up for her only ever made matters worse.

"Thank you, Frances, I believe you have encouraged Eleanor quite enough."

Aunt Frances dropped her chin and gazed at the floral tablecloth, her fingers sweeping at the crumbs that remained after breakfast. Ellie could see she was biting her tongue. The muscle in her jaw twitched with the effort.

"Mother, I'm sorry. It just slipped out of my fingers."

"And why do you suppose that happened? You were too busy arguing with me, your head full of these ridiculous notions your aunt insists on feeding you. . ."

"No, that's not why. . ." Ellie burst out, then trailed off. She felt her face flushing. Her mother was *always* so angry with her, no matter what she did. . . But a quiet voice inside murmured that it was also true. She had been too rough as she picked up the plate, annoyed with her mother for interrupting her conversation with Aunt Frances. Annoyed – if she was honest with herself – that

2

she was having to clear away the breakfast things in the first place. Her mother never did anything.

"Why must you always disagree with everything I say?" Mother continued. "You know it's true – I can see on your face. And you have only proved my point. Your best hope is to marry well, and for that you must learn to perform simple household tasks. *And* you must learn obedience. There is no use in making these grand and, frankly, ludicrous plans."

Ellie felt a fresh wave of anger flood her, her guilt over the plate forgotten.

"But why? Why is finding a man my best hope? Look at Aunt Frances. She's made a success of her life without having to marry."

Aunt Frances gave her an encouraging smile, but her mother was ready with her retort, her mouth twisted into something ugly and cruel-looking.

"And that is the sort of future you want for yourself, is it? Scrabbling for money as a bank clerk, living in poky digs in Brighton with no husband or children. . ."

"Mother!"

"It's all right, Ellie." Aunt Frances's calm voice

cut across the argument, and Ellie felt another great wave of love for her. "I assure you, Josephine, I'm very happy with my life and my choices. But I'm not suggesting that Ellie imitate them – what I'm saying to her is that she has any number of opportunities. . ."

"Oh, there you go again. You are doing the child no favours, Frances, merely setting her up for disappointment. And I'll thank you not to interfere in my conversation with my daughter. Your brother indulges her enough as it is."

For someone who spent so much time in bed with mystery illnesses and bouts of nerves and energy loss, it was amazing how her mother could become so suddenly animated, Ellie mused. She longed to argue back, to suggest that her father encouraged her because he loved her and wanted to see her happy, not stuck in a house in tiny Endstone for the rest of her life, carrying out boring domestic tasks that she would never be good at, and breaking any number of plates! Father didn't believe there was only one life for girls. But she knew that her mother would never back down, never agree with her.

"Besides which, Eleanor," Mother continued, her

voice rising again as though she scented victory, "what makes you think you'd be happy in a profession such as your aunt's? You're the one constantly moaning about how boring you find school!"

Once again Ellie's resolve not to answer back wavered in the face of this injustice. "But, Mother, that's because all they teach us at school – well, us girls, at least – is how to knit and run a household. It's pointless, and you know how hopeless I am at knitting!"

"You consider your laziness and ineptitude some sort of excuse, do you? How precisely do you intend to feed and clothe yourself and your family without those skills?"

"But, I mean, *you*. . ." Ellie saw the dangerous look in her mother's eyes and trailed off again. No, it was not wise to point out how little Mother did around the house.

Her mother watched her for a moment, grey eyes level, waiting to see if she would dare to say more. Ellie kept her own gaze fixed on the floor, her jaw clenched tight, locking the words inside.

"I don't know what I did wrong with you, Eleanor,

I really don't. Perhaps I haven't been firm enough. As it is, you're running wild. Don't look at me like that! What else am I supposed to think when you arrive home late looking like some sort of vagabond?"

"I told you what happened!" Ellie couldn't help herself. "I left my pocket watch at home because I didn't want to get it wet. And our boat drifted further in the current than we realized. And Jack said—"

"Yes, *Jack*," her mother cut in, her nostrils flaring as though she had detected an unpleasant smell. "That good-for-nothing factory boy. How entirely unsurprising that he should be behind this latest misbehaviour." Her mother had never approved of Ellie's friendship with Jack.

"It wasn't—"

"How you could imagine fishing is a suitable activity for a young lady is beyond me."

Aunt Frances had been silent for some time now. Arguing came no more naturally to her than it did to Ellie. But now she raised her calm voice in Ellie's defence. "Well, I think fishing is a perfectly wholesome activity. Fresh air, nature. . . And last night's fish was delicious."

Ellie's shoulders slumped. She hadn't told her mother where the fish had come from. When Alice, their maid, had still worked for them, Ellie had often brought back fish from her expeditions for her to cook. Now that they'd had to let Alice go, it had become harder to smuggle it in. She'd thought she'd got away with it on this occasion, but one glance at her mother's expression told her otherwise.

Ellie's mind wandered back to the afternoon spent with her friend. They'd eaten their sandwiches lying on their backs in the boat, before being startled by tugs on their lines so sudden that they nearly capsized. They'd burned their cheekbones and noses that afternoon, then as the sun got lower they had had a small bonfire on the riverfront. Nothing her mother said could ruin the memory for her. Nothing could make Jack less worthy in her eyes.

A thin wail came from the direction of the stairs. It was Ellie's baby brother, Charlie.

Aunt Frances, still quailing under Mother's glower, leapt to her feet. "I'll go to him," she said hastily, and hurried from the room.

Mother took a breath and Ellie knew she was

preparing to launch into a fresh round of accusations, but she was interrupted by the sound of the front door.

Father!

Ellie saw a slight softening of her mother's face and they both turned towards the kitchen door in time to see her father stride in. Normally he would pause in the hallway to put down his briefcase and take off his jacket, but today he carried both as he burst into the kitchen, his eyes bright, cheeks flushed, brandishing a newspaper.

"Wesley. . . ?" Mother began.

"My girls! What a historic day!" Ellie's father kissed his wife on the cheek and then pulled Ellie into a rough embrace, throwing the newspaper down on to the table.

"What do you mean, Father?"

"We're at war, my darling."

"War?" The word sounded heavy in the room.

Father gestured towards the table, where the headline screamed 'ENGLAND READY FOR WAR!'

Of course. In all the drama of the morning, Ellie had forgotten that the country was awaiting news from London. The Prime Minister had issued an ultimatum to the German Kaiser Wilhelm II, insisting that he move his troops out of Belgium immediately, or Britain and Germany would be at war. The Kaiser had given his answer today.

"Yes, indeed. We have been left with no choice. It would be shameful to stand aside any longer. We must do the honourable thing."

We? Ellie thought. Somehow she couldn't connect what went on in distant countries, which she knew only as coloured shapes on a map, with her own life. Even London, where the politicians had been debating the issue for weeks, felt like another world.

Frances re-entered the room, carrying a smiling, if tear-stained, Charlie in her arms. Her normally pink cheeks looked oddly grey.

"So this is it then? We're at war with Germany."

Ellie's father strolled over to his sister and dropped a kiss on her forehead as he scooped up Charlie and tickled his tummy.

"Don't look so worried, old girl. Everyone says it will be all over by Christmas. You know we couldn't have stood by while the Kaiser took over the show. If we let him have his way in Europe he'll be after our Empire next. This is important. It's for Ellie and Charlie, so that their futures are protected."

There it was again. *Her future*. Ellie didn't know when her future had become so important to everyone. Including, it would seem, the Prime Minister.

Two

"Naturally, I intend to join up myself."

"The army?"

Her father's voice startled Ellie out of her reverie.

"Of course, my darling. Every man must do what he can."

"But you're needed here. Your patients need you. What will Endstone do without its doctor?"

I need you, Ellie wanted to say. How could she imagine life without her father?

"But I am needed all the more over in Europe. I can't leave it to the other fellows. Everyone will have people and responsibilities that they are leaving behind – we can't ask others to do what we refuse to do ourselves. We must think of the greater good."

Her father's eyes – blue like Aunt Frances' and like Charlie's – were fixed on some distant point, as though he'd already left her far behind. Ellie glanced at her mother, whose face looked more pinched than ever.

"You'll remember this day for ever, Ellie," her father went on, jiggling Charlie in his arms. "Our country is standing up and doing what is right. We're at war."

"I still don't understand. Why is it up to England to make the Germans get out of Belgium?"

"Because we're Belgium's allies, Ellie," said Aunt Frances. She twisted a strand of her short, curly hair around her finger as she spoke. "We've sworn to support and defend each other. And if we don't stand by our promises to our allies when they need our help, well, who will support us should we ever need it?"

"I see," said Ellie, but really she didn't. All these countries – Austria-Hungary, Serbia, Belgium – they felt so far away. How could things that happened over there mean that her father had to leave? It all seemed so strange.

"You understand, don't you, my clever girl?" Ellie's father was looking so proudly at her. She couldn't let him down.

"Of course," she lied.

"It won't be up to the chaps alone, Ellie," Aunt Frances went on. "There will be things we can do to help too. And as your father says, all the talk is that the whole thing will be over by Christmas. He'll be back before you know it." She sounded as though she were trying to convince herself just as much as Ellie.

"This is all well and good," Ellie's mother cut in, "but there's no point getting overexcited before we know all the particulars. In my view, we've had more than enough theatricals for one morning. And the table is not going to lay itself, Ellie!"

After lunch, Ellie's father went back to work. Ellie cleared away the lunch things without any more breakages and settled Charlie down for his nap. Her mother had taken to her bed with a headache, leaving Ellie in no doubt as to whom she considered responsible for the housework and babysitting.

Ellie took the water from the dishes out to the garden to pour over the vegetable patch. It was a warm day, though she could see dark clouds in the distance, and a pleasant breeze lifted her hair from her clammy neck and carried the smell of wild garlic and seaweed from the nearby shore. Ellie gazed towards the sea which stretched out beyond the cliff, into the distance. A small boat, painted a cheerful red, its sail puffed proudly in the wind, drifted along beneath the cliff.

Everything suddenly felt so strange and unfamiliar. Even her own body felt like an uncomfortable dress she was forced to wear. She felt muffled, her senses blunted, as if she had a head cold coming on.

A quiet but unmistakeable squealing sound from the front of the house roused her from her thoughts. *Jack!*

Ellie hurried through the back door, dropping the bucket for the dishes into the kitchen and skidding into the hallway in time to see Aunt Frances opening the door.

Jack's wary expression disappeared immediately on seeing Aunt Frances and was replaced by a broad grin. His bicycle – owner of the squeaky brakes – lay abandoned on its side by the front door, its back wheel still spinning. His hair was wilder than ever.

"Hello, Miss Phillips! Hello, Ellie! Mrs Phillips not around?"

"Sssh, she's sleeping, Jack! And we'd all like to keep it that way," giggled Ellie.

"Right you are," agreed Jack in a whisper that still sounded uncomfortably loud to Ellie.

Frances bustled them back into the kitchen. Jack was barely across the threshold when he burst out again. "You've heard, though, haven't you? You must have done! We're at war. War!"

"We've heard, Jack, yes," replied Aunt Frances. She closed the kitchen door firmly, leaning her slim frame against it as though that would further muffle the noise.

Ellie lifted the kettle on to the range. "You certainly seem happy about it," she remarked.

"Well, it's about time something happened around here! I'm going to sign up straight away. Do my bit and all that."

"Oh, Jack, you haven't changed at all!" Aunt Frances smiled at him, patting him on the shoulder. "You always wanted to play soldiers with Ellie, even when you were just a tiny boy, both of you in your little school uniforms"

"Yeah!" Jack gave one of his big, booming laughs and Ellie and Aunt Frances winced, glancing towards the door. "But Ellie always wanted to play explorers! Just think, El, finally I might have a chance to get out of this dump!"

Ellie's feeling of queasiness grew. Jack too! She would be stuck in Endstone with only her mother and Charlie. She loved her baby brother but he was too young to be much company.

As if reading her thoughts, Aunt Frances spoke up. "I'm sorry to disappoint you, Jack, but you're too young to join the army," she said gently.

"I'm fourteen!" Jack protested.

"You have to be eighteen Jack. And even then, with all the training I'd be surprised if they sent you away to fight for months."

Jack's face fell. Ellie felt sorry for him but also relieved. If the war was going to be over by Christmas, there was no chance Jack would go away. Good. At least she would not lose her friend as well as her father.

"You just want to dress up in a uniform and look like one of your toy soldiers," she teased as she handed him a cup. The dainty china vessel looked tiny in his large, calloused hand.

"I do not!" he replied hotly. "This isn't like our games when we were nippers, El! It's serious. We can't let the Hun take over Europe!"

"What do you care about what's happening on the other side of the English Channel, Jack?"

"I care! Of course I do! It's like . . . it's like. . ." He struggled for a moment, brow furrowed. "It's like when Endstone are playing Littlecompton at the footie. And when Littlecom start acting as though they own the place. . ." His voice trailed off. "No, no, it's not like that." He tried again. "It's . . . it's important, El! It's not a joke!"

"He's right," Aunt Frances said quietly, gazing into her cup as though she could see something more than her tea in there. "I don't like war. You're both too young to remember the Boer Wars, but I knew plenty of good men from home who went away and. . ." She glanced at Ellie and paused. "But we have to stand up for what we believe in. We can't allow Germany to occupy countries that don't belong to her. We can't let our allies down."

"I know, I know we can't. It's just. . . Everything's already changing. . ." Ellie said.

"And haven't you been longing for things to change, Miss 'I'm Going to Travel the World'?" Jack winked, his customary broad smile back in place on his freckled face.

"I suppose I have. . ."

"Goodness!" Aunt Frances suddenly exclaimed, glancing at the clock on the wall. "If I don't get a move on, I'm going to miss my train."

"Back to Brighton today, Miss Phillips?" Jack enquired.

"Yes, I'm afraid so," Frances replied. "My leave is over and I'm back in work tomorrow."

Ellie knew that her aunt would be secretly pleased to get back to her job and her friends. She would be more in need of a holiday from Mother than she'd ever been from work. Ellie imagined her aunt returning to her room in her digs. She had never been allowed to visit, but in her mind it was tidy and organized, yet filled with books and pictures and Frances's understated but stylish clothes, with a desk for her to sit at and write her letters. Frances was an enthusiastic and entertaining correspondent. It was the one good thing about her living so far away.

"We'll see you off at the station, won't we, Jack? Then we can go into the village."

"Course! I'll take your bag on my bicycle, Miss Phillips."

After checking that her mother and Charlie were both still sleeping, Ellie retrieved her bicycle from the shed and the three of them set off – Ellie and Jack wheeled their bikes so that Aunt Frances could keep up.

It was an easy twenty-minute stroll to the station, down a pretty lane lined with hedgerows. They met no one to delay them. Reaching the village, the path ran behind the main square, but there were few houses on this side and it tended to be quiet.

All too soon they were there, Jack passed Aunt Frances's bag to one of the porters, who loaded it on to the train. There weren't many other travellers on a weekday afternoon and they stood chatting on the little platform, waiting for the whistle.

"I wish I could go with you," said Ellie. The train station always filled her with a longing to go somewhere – anywhere! She sometimes passed by on her bicycle just to study the train timetables and imagine the adventures she might have. How exciting it would be to pack a neat suitcase like Aunt Frances' and head off to explore unknown towns and cities!

"Oh, so do I, my dear! You would love Brighton. We could go to the theatre and eat ices by the sea. How you would love the Pavilion! It makes one feel as though one were in India. Maybe you could come in the Christmas holidays. Though we might have tea rather than ices then!"

"Maybe," said Ellie doubtfully. It sounded wonderful, but she knew that her mother would never allow it.

The stationmaster blew the whistle and Aunt Frances boarded the train, giving hasty kisses first to Ellie, then to Jack, causing him to blush fiercely.

"Goodbye!" she called, her head emerging from the window. A smile lit her face and made her look no older than Ellie. "I expect war will be all over by the time I see you next!"

Ellie and Jack stood and waved until the train was out of sight, then picked up their bicycles and set off for the centre of the village.

Jack glanced at Ellie, who was still deep in thought,

already missing her aunt, thinking about how different their lives might become between now and Christmas. "I'll race you," he yelled suddenly, standing up on his pedals to build up momentum for a burst of speed.

Ellie eyes brightened and her broodings were forgotten. "You never learn, do you, Jack Scott?"

The pair tore down the main road leading into the village. Jack's longer legs were an advantage, but Ellie was lighter, and experienced from years of competing with him. She seemed almost to fly across the square and skidded to a halt by the little fountain at least five seconds before him, red-cheeked and gasping for breath.

Old Miss Webb was emerging from the village store, bent double, her basket weighted down with tins. Ellie had only just managed to swerve to avoid her. Jack's equally dramatic arrival seconds later was too much.

"Heaven preserve me! Is it not enough that the Germans are coming to murder me in my bed? The pair of you are determined to run me down in the road and spare them the trouble!"

"Sorry, Miss Webb," Ellie mumbled, trying to

ignore the delighted grin she knew would be beaming from Jack's face.

"Sorry, are you? Master Scott doesn't look very sorry. I don't know why your mother lets you run wild, Eleanor, I really don't. . ."

They watched her shuffle off, muttering under her breath. Ellie sighed. The last thing she needed was a complaint getting back to her mother. It would be yet another excuse to keep Ellie at home and away from Jack. Another example of why her daughter needed to behave in a more ladylike fashion.

But then her mother never came into the village, and she thought the likes of Miss Webb far beneath her. There was little chance of them speaking.

"Well, Eleanor, I don't know what we're going to do with you," Jack teased, his dark eyebrows high on his forehead. "Running wild! It's the talk of the village!"

"You be quiet, *Master* Scott! You're the one who nearly sent her toppling into the fountain!"

"Into the fountain, you say?" Jack asked innocently, with a glance in the direction of the splashing water behind Ellie's back.

"Don't even think about it!" she squealed, hurrying

to safety through the door of the village store and setting the bell jingling as she did so. "I'm going to tell your mother!"

She came face to face with a queue of curious faces, and flushed deeply.

"What are you going to tell me?" Mrs Scott was behind the counter, holding out a handful of change to Mrs Bridge. Her kind face looked tired but a smile flickered at the corner of her mouth.

"Oh, nothing, sorry."

Jack was still chuckling as he joined her. They stood by the newspaper rack, jostling each other and sniggering as Mrs Scott served the rest of the customers.

When finally there was a lull, Mrs Scott called them over.

"I hope you're behaving yourself, Jack!"

"I always do, Mam," he replied, planting a kiss on her rosy cheek.

As she beamed up at him, Ellie realized that Jack was a whole head taller than his mother now.

"I don't know about that!" She tucked a strand of hair – auburn, liberally shot through with grey – behind her ear. "Well, big news, eh? War! Feels like the whole village has been in, wanting to talk about it. Then there's some like poor old Miss Webb who thinks she's got to buy up the whole shop before the Germans come marching down the street! This is about the first break I've had all day!"

Ellie and Jack caught each other's eye and burst out laughing all over again.

"You two should be nice to poor Miss Webb. She's a lonely old thing."

Suddenly the church bells started to ring across the square, making all three of them jump. They moved to stand in the doorway in time to see a group of older village lads marching past in a rough semblance of a formation of soldiers, whistling "It's a Long Way to Tipperary". A gaggle of smaller boys, including Jack's little brother George, followed in their wake, blowing whistles and banging drums. George turned and waved when he saw them, before returning to his furious drumming.

"Goodness knows where he got that thing!" Mabel Scott laughed.

More and more people were spilling out into the square, drawn by the commotion and the promise of gossip. Before long most of the village was there. It felt like Christmas. Voices thrummed, shouts and laughter punctured the air.

Ellie felt a wave of excitement coursing through her, which turned into giddiness as Jack seized her by the waist and spun her round and round until they were both laughing hysterically. As he set her down, the familiar faces danced and swam before her eyes, the square tilting tipsily as though she were on a fairground ride.

Jack was right. She had wanted something to happen – something that mattered – for so long. And here it was at last!

Three

"Come on then, Ellie. We've got a couple of hours before dinner and I want to make the most of them."

Ellie glanced once more at her mother, still expecting her permission to be withdrawn. But for once she hadn't been able to find fault with Ellie's chores, and she struggled to remain disagreeable in the face of her husband's enthusiasm.

"Off you go then. But I want you home to help with Charlie's bath later." Her expression was cool but at least she didn't seem annoyed.

Ellie didn't need to be told again. She barrelled past her father and out into the sunshine, feeling as though she'd escaped from prison.

Her father followed, laughing, then hurried to the shed to pull out their bicycles.

"You're even keener than me, I think!"

Ellie smiled at him but didn't reply. She had tried often enough to talk to her father about Mother. He was sympathetic, but he just didn't understand. Ellie knew how much he loved her mother and she expected that was why he couldn't grasp her frustration. And she hated to upset him.

"What are you thinking about, old girl?" her father asked as he passed her bicycle over, lightly knocking on the top of her head with his knuckles as he did so.

"Nothing." She beamed at him again. Ellie liked nothing better than to spend time alone with her father, to get him all to herself. "Where shall we go first?"

"Let's call by the library to see who's there. Then, though it pains me to say it, I think at this hour on a Friday, the pub might be our best bet."

As they pedalled past leafy hedgerows, under arching tree branches and into the village – at a much more sedate pace than when she was with Jack – Ellie asked her father more about the war, what had led to it and what it would mean for them all. They had begun to talk about it many times before at home, but Mother always said that Ellie was involving herself in things that didn't concern her. It was easier when she wasn't there.

Now, as they rode along Father attempted an explanation of the events that had caused the war: complex alliances between the European powers, the growing threat of German military might and the assassination of Archduke Ferdinand in Serbia. It was all a bit of a mess, he admitted that, but he was very clear that Britain owed a duty to her friends to stand beside them against the bullying of the Kaiser. It was simply the right thing to do.

As he had promised, Father had signed up to join the army at the earliest opportunity and had spent every spare moment going round the village urging the other local men to do the same. Ellie still couldn't bear the thought of him leaving, but he was certainly persuasive. She had begun to wish she could join up herself, rather than being stuck at home, left behind as usual.

As they approached the library, Ellie recognized Jack's lanky frame standing outside. He was staring fixedly at something on the wall. Ellie and her father called out to him. Jack glanced round for long enough to throw a distracted wave in their direction, before turning back to look at the wall. As they pulled up behind him, they saw that the object of his intense concentration was a huge poster bearing the face of Lord Kitchener, the famous army officer, his expression fierce beneath his bushy brow and moustache, his finger stabbing out towards them.

BRITONS! YOUR COUNTRY NEEDS YOU! it proclaimed.

Without taking his eyes away, Jack whispered, "I swear, he's pointing right at me!"

Ellie's father laughed loudly, clapping Jack on the back. "I don't think he can hear you, lad!"

The village library had been turned into a recruitment office for the army, and as they stood teasing Jack, the doors opened and Stephen Chase and Billie Farrow emerged. The two boys had been a few years ahead of Ellie and Jack at school, until they had left at twelve to start work in the factory. Jack had followed them when he turned twelve four years later. Since they left school, they'd got taller and broader;

Billie had an impressive shadow of stubble, while Stephen was never seen without a cigarette in hand (except when his mother was around). Nonetheless, they never seemed to Ellie to have changed much at all.

"Hello, Dr Phillips!" Billie exclaimed. He was the more chatty of the pair, popular among the young boys of the village, whose football team he coached. "We did like you said. We joined up!"

"Well done, lads, well done. All of Endstone will be very proud of you. All of England!"

Only Jack was scowling. "What changed your mind, Bill?" he asked. "You didn't seem particularly keen earlier!"

"When the doctor told us we could come back to the factory when the war's all over, it sounded all right. I don't want to be in the Army for ever!"

"When it's all over *or* after three years, whichever is the longer," Wesley corrected him.

"I think I can persuade my Moll to wait that long before we get married. Any longer, though, and she might give up on me!"

"Well, she must understand – and what would she think of you if you didn't go, eh, Billie?" Ellie's father was smiling but his eyes were serious. "Anyway, it should all be behind us by Christmas. She won't have much of a wait."

Jack was looking at them with such a wistful expression that Ellie felt a little of her earlier queasiness return.

"Don't look so worried, Jackie boy," Stephen joked, punching him playfully on the shoulder, "we'll have those Germans taken care of before you have to join up."

"But I *want* to join up!" Jack spluttered in protest.

"Come on, Jack, Ellie," Dr Phillips intervened, before Jack could get himself worked up again. "Let's call by The Dog and Duck and see if we can't recruit a few more soldiers there."

Endstone was such a tiny village that Jack often joked that you could stand outside one building and hit any of the others by throwing a coin. The pub was only a few yards away, across the square, a little closer to the sea front. Girls weren't allowed inside, so Ellie and Jack waited by the pretty, painted front door. They watched as Ellie's father entered the gloomy interior, through the blue fog of pipe smoke.

"Good afternoon, gentlemen!" he greeted them loudly.

"Afternoon, Wesley!"

"Good to see you again, Dr Phillips. I'm just on my way home from the recruitment office. Are you pleased with me?"

"Good man, Arthur, good man. But I think your home is the other way!"

A burst of raucous laughter drifted out to Ellie and Jack.

"He hasn't told the missus yet!" called one loud voice.

"Pint of porter, Doctor Phillips?"

"Well, I oughtn't to but . . . I suppose a half wouldn't hurt!"

"Course it wouldn't. Just what the doctor ordered, eh, Doctor?"

Ellie rolled her eyes, but Jack was still brooding.

"Those blokes think I'm a coward," he said gruffly.

"Who?"

"Billie and Steve."

"Don't be so silly. You're *too young*, Jack. They know your age as well as I do. You wouldn't be allowed!"

"It's so stupid, though. What's age got to do with it? I'm already as tall and strong as Will!"

"Well, what's *height* got to do with it, more to the point?" Ellie laughed, giving him a shove. But Jack did not respond. His gaze went over her head and into the pub behind her, his expression darkening.

Ellie whirled around to see a group of men shuffling uncomfortably around her father. In the smoky darkness at the far end of the bar she recognized Jack's father. His was the voice that they heard now as the others lapsed into an awkward silence.

"I'm wondering who the devil put you in charge of this whole operation, Doctor?" Mr Scott was perched on the very edge of his stool. "What makes you think you can go around bothering men who are tired after an honest week's work?"

Ellie heard Jack's sharp exhalation from behind her and her heart contracted with pity for him. At the same time, she felt her fists tightening as she watched how Mr Scott was looking at her father.

"No one put me in charge, Joe," Wesley began in a placating tone. His palms were turned towards Joe, his stance relaxed. "I'm just doing my bit to help, that's all. I'm sorry if I disturbed you."

"You *did* disturb me. You did! What makes you so superior, anyway?"

"Calm down, Joe." John, the landlord was frowning, shifting from foot to foot behind the bar. "You won't be getting any more pints in this establishment if you're going to carry on like that."

"What does he expect would happen if we all did like he said?" Joe clearly wasn't finished. His whole body seemed to vibrate with tension. "Who'd run the factory and work the farms, if we all upped and went to France?"

"Stop it, Dad. You're making a spectacle of yourself." Ellie hadn't noticed Jack's older brother, Will, until he appeared from the other side of the bar, where he'd been sitting with some other young men.

"Again," added Jack.

"Not to worry, lads, not to worry," Ellie's father said, his tone even. "I'd best be off home for tea, anyway. I'm sorry to have given offence, Joe."

Mr Scott grunted. He settled back on his bar stool as Dr Phillips rejoined Ellie and Jack outside.

They all looked at each other in silence for a moment. Before the silence could be broken, they were joined by Will.

"Dr Phillips, do you have a moment?" Will's freckled cheeks were still hot with embarrassment. "Oh, hello, Jack. Hello, Ellie."

"Don't you think you'd better get Dad home before he shames us all more?" said Jack, staring pointedly at his brother.

Will barely gave him a glance. "Can't you do it? I want to talk to Dr Phillips."

"Your father will be fine, boys. John will send him on his way soon. Now, what did you want to talk to me about, Will?"

"It's about the army, sir."

"What about it? And please don't call me sir."

The thought of referring to Ellie's father as anything other than sir seemed to momentarily flummox Will. It was a few seconds before he recovered himself sufficiently to continue.

"Er . . . yes, sir. Well, I mean. . ." He took a breath. "I'm going to join up. At least, I want to. At least, I think I do."

"For pity's sake," Jack growled, before Ellie shushed him.

"It's all right, Will. It's a daunting prospect, I know."

"I'm no coward, si— doctor."

Jack snorted.

"I want to do my bit, I really do. But . . . I know it won't be just playing soldiers, like Jack thinks."

"I do not!" Jack exploded.

Ellie took hold of his elbow to pull him away.

"Of course not," Dr Phillips said soothingly, somehow managing to make both brothers feel as though he were speaking to them. "No, it's not a game. You can be sure that the Germans will be taking it very seriously and so should you. There will be danger. But don't you face danger every day in the factory?"

"I suppose so."

"And this is an opportunity to be part of something big, something important – to change history. And to see something more of the world. I believe it could be the making of you, Will."

"Well, I suppose you're right."

"Of course he's right!" Jack bellowed. "Oh, it's

just not fair! If I were your age, Will, I wouldn't be standing around here wasting time and bothering Dr Phillips. I'd be first in line at the recruitment office!"

Ellie couldn't hold her thoughts in any longer. "You should think yourself lucky you're not a girl," she snapped. The three men looked at her in surprise. Jack was finally silent.

How she would love to see the world, to do something important. But even if she were old enough, still there would be no chance of adventure for her. She was stuck here, no matter what.

Four

Ellie seized Baby Charlie's small squirming form and carried him, still struggling, into the dark interior of the church. She shivered; even on a warm day at the height of summer, it was always so cold in here.

Charlie gave a happy squeal, as he always did when he remembered how the stone walls echoed his own voice back to him.

"Sssh, sshh," Ellie urged. Already she could see her mother's back stiffening as she walked up the aisle towards the pew where they always sat.

As Ellie shuffled on to the pew, her mother hissed, "*Please* try to keep him under control. It's humiliating to have him drowning out the reverend."

"I don't know why you don't look after him

yourself if I'm doing such a bad job," Ellie muttered under her breath.

"What was that?" her mother asked sharply, grey eyes narrowed.

"Nothing, Mother."

"Where has your father got to now?" her mother craned her neck – her tight bun set low against it – to locate Father, who was deep in conversation with Mr and Mrs Crouch. "Oh, honestly!"

Not for the first time, Ellie pondered how funny it was that her mother cared so much about appearances and was disliked by most of the villagers, while her father didn't care what anyone thought and was universally loved.

Eventually he joined them on their pew near the front, tickling Charlie and setting him squealing again, just as they rose for Reverend Chester.

Ellie wriggled uncomfortably in her stiff Sunday dress, which she had almost out grown, as the vicar began his sermon. Like everything else these days, it seemed, the subject was the war.

"And the people of Endstone are hugely proud that so many of our brave men have already signed up to go and fight for King and country. You will be in our thoughts and prayers every moment, as will all your fellow countrymen."

And in Germany too, Ellie found herself thinking. *Surely the Germans are praying to the same God to take care of their sons and brothers and make* them *victorious?* She was then surprised by the thought. *How can He choose? If He protects the soldiers on both sides then no one will ever win. But if He favours one, then He must not be listening to the prayers of the other.* She felt the start of a headache and tugged at the collar of her dress. Her mother glowered.

Ellie knew that she couldn't raise these questions with her parents, not even with her father. He was so convinced of the justice of going to war. Maybe he would consider it blasphemous to be thinking this way. She glanced at him. His expression was serious as he nodded along to the Reverend Chester's words.

Ellie's gaze wandered and came to rest on the motes of dust that hovered in the shafts of coloured light streaming through the stained glass windows. She had been coming to this church with her family every Sunday for her whole life. How strange to think that in a few weeks, she, her mother and Charlie would be here without her father. She shook away the thought. It wouldn't be for long, she told herself.

When the service was over, they filtered out into the watery daylight. Ellie looked past the square to the grey sea beyond. The breeze held the slightest mist of sea water; she could taste the salt on her lips. It was all so familiar; it looked just the same as always, yet everything was changing.

Her mother had cornered Reverend Chester and they were deep in conversation by the door of the church. He was the one villager she was always happy to speak with. Her father was talking to Will Scott. Will had signed up. They were leaving to begin their training in a matter of days.

Charlie was once again scampering around the gravestones at the side of the church. Ellie glanced anxiously at her mother, but she was still engrossed in conversation, so she felt safe letting her brother play. As she trailed behind Charlie, she passed the Parkes family, who owned one of the farms on the outskirts of the village. Mrs Parkes was red-faced, whispering urgently to their oldest son, Harry.

"Plenty of men are staying behind. I don't know why you're making such a fuss about it."

"Were you listening to that sermon?" Harry snapped in response, barely bothering to lower his voice. "It's my duty!"

"Your duty is to your family, to our business. . ."

Ellie kept walking, embarrassed to have eavesdropped on a family row, and wondering how many conversations like that were happening in families all over the country.

Back at home that afternoon, Ellie was playing with Charlie in the bedroom they shared. His soldiers were doing battle with her old porcelain doll, who was a giant next to them. Charlie didn't really understand the details of the game, but he loved it when she made his soldiers shout, "Charge!" and gallop towards the poor besieged doll.

"Daddy's going to be just like one of your soldiers, Charlie. He's going to be a real hero."

"Dada!" Charlie agreed solemnly, before removing the soldier from Ellie's hand, clearly feeling she wasn't playing right. As he thudded it around the floor with his right hand, his left, clutching his tattered teddy, crept towards his mouth. He was teething again.

Ellie's laughter died in her throat as she heard voices raised from downstairs.

". . .want to? But you must see that there's no other choice."

Her father.

Ellie shuffled closer to her open door in time to hear her mother's voice in response.

". . .simply concerned about what will happen to your practice and your patients here. You have responsibilities to them too, you know, Wesley."

"Of course I do. I know I do. But I have a responsibility to set an example. And Thomas won't be joining up – not through lack of trying, poor chap, but it's an impossibility with that leg of his."

"Thomas is barely out of medical school," Mother replied, her voice becoming shrill in a way that was all too familiar to Ellie. "To all intents and purposes, he is still your apprentice."

"He is a very competent doctor. He simply needs an opportunity to prove himself. I think this will be an ideal chance for him to develop."

Her mother began to speak again, but her father cut across her. "And I would like you to support him in this, Josephine, let him know that you are available for whatever practical help or advice he may need."

"Me?"

"Yes. We must all do our bit."

"So you keep saying. But I hardly know what practical help I could offer."

"Oh, I think after being a doctor's wife for fourteen years, you know as much as, if not more than, me."

Ellie could hear the teasing smile creeping into her father's voice. He obviously felt the conversation was over.

Not so her mother. "I'm already trying to cope with running the household without Alice. Now we're to make do without you, *and* you want me help Thomas."

"Frances will be here as often as she can." He ignored the loud – and rather unladylike, thought Ellie – harrumphing sound from his wife. "And our little Ellie, of course."

Ellie moved away from the door before she could hear her mother's response to this. There were some things she didn't need to listen to. But her head was buzzing with questions. Where exactly would her father be going? He'd told her he would be in a foot regiment, but what did that mean? Would it be dangerous?

Of course it will be dangerous, she thought, *the Germans will be shooting at him. Why would they care that he is a doctor and a good man?*

There was a sharp tug at her ankle. She looked down to see Charlie thrusting a soldier at her, a fierce scowl on his round face.

"Sorry, Charlie!" she sighed, re-entering her own miniature battlefield.

Five

A motorbus was parked in front of the library, its engine purring. It was a deep red, polished to a shine; a thing of beauty, agreed the crowd of villagers gathered around it. Some of the braver children – Jack's brother George included – crept aboard when the driver wasn't watching, giggling and then shushing each other noisily.

At the heart of the throng were the eleven men who had signed up, arms around wives, children on their shoulders, or being fussed over by mothers. And yet, Ellie thought, they somehow seemed separate, already far away. That was how she felt about Father.

If anyone else felt that way, they were doing a good job of hiding it. The holiday atmosphere that had underlined everything since the outbreak of war was still alive. Cheerful bunting was strung across the square, children were waving Union Jacks a hastily assembled band were belting out popular tunes such as "The Girl I Left Behind Me". Jack was among them, playing his fiddle with such vigour and enthusiasm as though he thought this performance might convince them to let him join up on the spot. Even the weather was adding to the feel of a picnic or summer party; the sun was shining and there was only the gentlest breeze from the seafront.

Slowly, the men began to board the motorbus, duffel bags slung over their shoulders. Mrs Anderson, who was expecting her first baby, started to cry softly as her husband made his way to a seat, waving as he went.

Jack's mother put an arm around her. "Now, now, my love," she said in bouncy tones that didn't match the furrow between her eyebrows, "there's nothing to cry about. He'll be back and under your feet again before you even have time to miss him!"

At a word from Jack, the band began to play "Land of Hope and Glory", and the crowd joined in.

As Billie Farrow boarded, he swung around on the handrail, bellowing at his fiancée, "Best set a date for a Christmas wedding, Moll! The war'll be over and I'll get some leave for a honeymoon!"

This was greeted by a rowdy cheer from the men on the bus.

"See you under the mistletoe," she replied with a grin, causing whoops and calls to go up from the crowd.

Ellie's father had been circulating through the throng, making time to talk to everyone. He clapped his young colleague, Thomas, on the shoulder and shook his hand enthusiastically. The young man had only just arrived in Endstone. He stood on the edge of the crowd, blinking anxiously through his thick glasses at anyone who looked his way.

Dr Phillips returned to his family, standing a little away from the crowd. As usual, Ellie wished her mother wouldn't keep herself so apart, and seem to look down her nose so at all the others. What if people thought Ellie was the same?

She watched her mother give her father a cool peck on the cheek and felt an unfamiliar pang of sympathy.

Her mother's face looked so pale and pinched. No doubt the other villagers saw it as pride or coldness or irritation, but Ellie could detect real fear in her mother's darting eyes.

Her father shook her from her thoughts as he swept her into his arms, hugging her tight. Crushed into his jacket, with his familiar smell engulfing her, Ellie felt a wave of panic rising up her throat, threatening to choke her.

"When are you going to France?" she managed to stammer.

"I told you, darling girl, I don't know exactly. Probably in a few weeks' time, after we've completed our training."

They'd had this same conversation many times since he'd signed up. It was as though imprinting the details on her mind would keep her father closer by her side.

"Till then you'll be in Aldershot?" She looked up at the lines around his eyes, the deep set dimples in his cheeks.

"I'll be in Aldershot," he agreed patiently. She was clinging on to his lapels now. She had a hundred questions, and if she didn't ask them now she wouldn't get another chance. But she knew she had asked them all before.

He pulled her in close again and murmured into her hair. "You'll look after Mother, won't you? I know she can be a bit hard on you sometimes, but she's not as tough as she likes to pretend."

Ellie wondered about that but she nodded into his chest, "I will."

"That's enough now, you two," her mother interrupted sharply. Ellie and her father exchanged a smile. "The other men are waiting for you. There's no need to make a scene."

"You're right, my dear, as always." He leaned into the pram to ruffle Charlie's fair hair. "I'll be back in no time. Take care!"

With a last wave, he made his way through the crowd and climbed on to the bus. The driver clambered into his seat and started the engine, causing the smaller children to cheer with delight.

Slowly the bus pulled away. Ellie watched her father joking with the other men. There was a deep, dragging ache in her chest. She glanced at her mother, whose shoulders looked stiffer than ever, her expression curiously frozen. Ellie felt a sudden urge to reach out and touch her, maybe even hug her. But she resisted, imagining her mother's reaction. Still, perhaps her father was right. Mother wasn't as strong as she liked to pretend. His leaving would affect her more than anyone. At least Ellie had Jack and her other friends. Mother kept everyone at a distance, even little Charlie.

Ellie resolved to do all that she could to keep her mother happy from now on. No more arguing back. She would help out more around the house – as boring as it was. She nodded to herself. Everyone was having to do their part for the war effort and this would be hers. It would make Father happy when he came home at Christmas too.

It was at this point that her mother swung sharply round, all trace of vulnerability gone from her face.

"Stop gawping, Eleanor, and straighten your dress – you look like one of the factory girls!"

Ellie clenched her jaw. She felt her resolve sliding away like a dribble of milk on Charlie's chin. She strode away to join Jack's mother and sister Anna still standing in the crowd. They greeted her with sad smiles.

Behind them, Jack was talking to the other musicians, laughing despite all his earlier complaints about being left behind. Ellie noticed that his father had not arrived to see Will off, but she knew better than to mention it.

It was as though Mrs Scott had read her mind though. "Of course, Joe would have been here if he could have. He couldn't get away from the factory. I'm sure he's ever so proud of our Will, though."

"Are you?" said Anna with a raised eyebrow. "That's not what he said to me."

Mrs Scott hushed her hastily, her cheeks flaming. "That's enough out of you," she hissed. "Go and get your little brother, before he tries to run away again."

Anna sauntered off, tossing her copper-coloured hair, and Mrs Scott and Ellie exchanged a smile, before looking back in the direction of the departing bus that was taking their men away from them.

For Endstone, the war had truly begun.

Six

Ellie woke early on her first day back at school, pushing back the coverlet with unusual enthusiasm and almost skipping to the basin to splash her face.

She was not normally so happy to go to school. She found it desperately dull most of the time, often wondering if there were some kind of conspiracy to keep all interesting knowledge from the pupils. But anything had to be better than being cooped up in the house day after day, missing her father, wondering where he was and what he was doing.

In the weeks since he had left, Ellie had done her very best to keep her promise to herself by helping her mother as much as she could, and not arguing with her. But if Mother had noticed the difference, she certainly wasn't letting it show. If anything, her temper was shorter than ever, when she was speaking at all. She claimed agonizing headaches almost every day, and these sent her to her room, leaving Ellie to look after Charlie. Ellie loved her little brother, but he couldn't speak whole sentences yet and she was beginning to feel she was losing her mind, from all the one-sided conversations and repetitive games and songs he demanded.

Jack often called by after he finished at the factory and Ellie longed to go with him down to the river, the seafront or just into the village. But she couldn't leave Charlie and she certainly couldn't manage with the pram or a wobbly-legged toddler in tow. Charlie's forehead already had one fading bruise from a tumble on the cobblestones. The weather had held and it felt like torture staring out of the window and thinking about all the adventures she might be having. Normally the summer holidays were a time for freedom and wildness – at least as much as she could get away with behind her mother's back. This year she had felt more imprisoned than during term time.

Before she left for school, Ellie got Charlie his breakfast, and made some toast for her mother, which she and Charlie took to her in her bedroom. She was pleased to see that her mother was up and dressed, pinning her long, silvery hair into a bun.

As so often in the past, Ellie worried about leaving Charlie alone with her mother. But delaying wouldn't make it any easier. Kissing her brother on the cheek she ran back down the stairs, grabbed her worn leather satchel and swept through the door. She seized her bicycle from where it was propped against the fence and bumped down the steep and stony path that led down towards the seafront.

When she reached the bottom, the path levelled out into a smoother track than ran along the beach. After so many days indoors, the fresh sea breeze felt wonderful against her hot, tight skin, and it lifted her hair off her sticky neck. As she cycled along the length of Big Beach (as the locals called it, though it wasn't really big enough to merit the name), she glanced to the left, across the sea. If she could fly across the Channel in a straight line, it would take her to France, to her father. She felt as though maybe, if she could just get up enough speed she might take flight. She lifted her left hand from the handlebars and let it coast on the breeze like a hovering seagull.

They had received several letters from Father while he was in Aldershot, one enclosing a photograph of him posing with some of the other men in their crisp new uniforms. In them he had written that they would be shipping out soon. But there had been nothing since he arrived in France. Ellie had hoped that he might come home before shipping out – Will and some of the other men had been back briefly – but sadly her father hadn't returned to Endstone before leaving for France.

Sometimes it felt as though he'd been gone for ever. On the other hand, sometimes Ellie would wake up in the morning and forget that he wasn't just down the hallway in her parents' bedroom.

"Come home soon, Father!" she cried towards the waves, the wind tearing the words out of her throat, her dark brown hair snapping and whipping around her face like the rigging on the fishing boats.

She put on an extra burst of speed for the last minutes of the journey and swerved to a halt in front of the school. Catching a glimpse of herself in the classroom window, she saw that her cheeks were pink and her hair more bedraggled than her mother would have tolerated.

Miss Smith, who taught the girls was waiting by the door. She gave Ellie a smile as she stowed her bicycle, though one eyebrow was raised.

"Welcome back, Eleanor. I see the holidays have done little to calm you down."

Ellie tugged her fingers through her hair in a vain attempt to tame it. Miss Smith was not as strict as Ellie's mother, but Ellie knew she didn't really approve of her unladylike behaviour. And although her teacher was kind-hearted, Ellie struggled to see anything of use in her lessons.

Sure enough, any hope that school might provide a pleasant break from the tedium at home was swiftly quashed.

"Now, girls, settle down please. This term we're going to be focusing on what we can do to help the war effort."

Ellie sat up in her seat, eyes wide with hope.

"We're going to be knitting clothes for the troops, to keep our boys warm in the cold months ahead in France."

Ellie's shoulders slumped. Knitting! Of all the pointless tasks school inflicted, knitting was the worst! Not only was it dull, but she had never managed to master it, so it was always incredibly frustrating. Was this really the most useful thing they could do?

"Hats, gloves, scarves," Miss Smith continued, pacing back and forth at the front of the room as though she were reciting poetry. "As many as we can. This is going to be a whole school effort."

"The boys too, miss?" Ellie asked.

Miss Smith sighed, pausing in her march. "I suppose there's little point in me asking you to raise your hand before you speak, Eleanor?"

"Sorry, miss." Ellie grinned, belatedly raising her hand.

"The boys may do it too, if they wish. Though I somehow doubt. . ."

"But they don't have to, miss?" Ellie insisted, her hand still in the air. She could feel some of the other girls shifting impatiently, rolling their eyes and muttering.

"No, they don't have to. They have other work to do."

"Couldn't I do the other work, miss? You know I'm no good at knitting. . ."

"Eleanor, I don't know why you always have to be so difficult. I should have thought you would want to do something for the war effort, with your own father over there in France."

"I do, miss. . ."

"Well, then, *please*, let's have no more fuss."

"Yes, miss. I'm sorry," Ellie mumbled. She knew the other girls saw her as a troublemaker, and she hated it. But she could never quite seem to stop herself. She so desperately wanted to learn about real, interesting things, things that would help her to escape Endstone and the life her mother had planned for her.

Miss Smith darted about the room, distributing knitting needles and the girls were allowed to select wool and patterns from a collection on the teacher's desk. The wool, Miss Smith explained, had been kindly salvaged from unwanted clothes or donated by some of the well-to-do ladies of Canterbury, the nearest major city.

Ellie trudged to the front of the classroom, trying to tell herself that this was her chance to contribute something from the home front, to do something worthwhile. Maybe her father would be the one to receive what she made and it would keep him warm and remind him of home.

With this in mind, she selected a royal blue, which would match the colour of his eyes. She was idly flicking through the patterns for a pair of mittens when a dainty hand appeared and plucked them from her grasp. She looked up.

"I think it's probably best if you stick to something simple, like a scarf, don't you?" Miss Smith said, not unkindly.

Ellie flushed and nodded, taking the simple pattern the teacher was holding out to her. She returned to her desk, peering at the instructions.

"What are you making, then?" asked Anna Scott, leaning over, her hair in a thick braid over one shoulder. Her own needles were already flying away in a blur of scarlet, though she barely glanced at them.

"Scarf," Ellie muttered.

"Coo, surely you don't need a pattern for a scarf? It's the simplest thing there is!"

"Not for me."

Anna laughed, gaily, returning to her work.

Ellie picked up her needles. She imagined her father in his garrison in France. She pictured him receiving a package, tearing it open in that hurried way that always made Josephine tut. He would pull out the beautiful blue scarf and immediately wind it round his neck. He would know at once it was from Ellie – maybe she could knit a secret message into it for him!

"Oh, Ellie, what have you done?" It was Miss Smith. Ellie followed the teacher's gaze towards her knitting. It was twisted and uneven, a different number of stitches on each of the three rows she had completed.

"Here, give it to me."

Ellie passed the knitting over mutely and watched as Miss Smith pulled out the rows. "Try again. You just need to pay a bit more attention."

"Away with the fairies again, Ellie?" Anna giggled.

Ellie knew she didn't mean it nastily, but to her embarrassment she felt a sudden wave of emotion.

"May I visit the lavatory, Miss?"

"Oh, you really should wait until morning break. . ." Miss Smith registered the tears hovering on Ellie's lower lashes. "Go on, then, be quick."

Ellie barely made it out of the classroom before the tears began flow. Once safely out of earshot she let herself sob freely, her frustrations, her sadness and her fears finally pouring out. Even when her tears were spent she stayed in the girl's lavatories, unable to re-face her class.

Ellie was glad to escape when school was finished. But as she cycled back along the beach front, the thought of returning home to her mother's claustrophobic silence and only Charlie for company was unbearable. Jack would be able to cheer her up but it was days since she had seen him, and he would still be working at the factory for a couple more hours.

At the turn-off for her house, Ellie glanced in its direction, before continuing straight along the path as it skirted the outside of the main village square. She would go to the surgery and see how Thomas was getting on, she decided.

Her father's surgery sat a little way behind the main square and could be reached via the church graveyard, which gave rise to gloomy jokes among some of the older villagers. It was the only surgery serving several villages in the surrounding area, as well as the farms outside them.

Ellie propped her bicycle against the front gate and walked along the path. As soon as she pushed the door open, she could tell something was wrong. The tiny waiting room was crammed with five adult patients and a wailing baby, all looking extremely grumpy. Her father never had more than one person waiting. Ellie didn't recognize the two men or the young mother with the infant, whom she guessed must be from outside Endstone, but the other patients were heavily pregnant Mrs Anderson and Miss Webb.

"All day we've been waiting for that young doctor!" Miss Webb burst out angrily. "All day, or near as makes no odds!" She broke into a spluttering cough, which caused the young mother to wrinkle her nose and edge further away – not easy given the size of the room.

"The Germans will be arriving any day now, any minute! And here I am, wasting my last moments in the wretched doctor's surgery." Miss Webb punctuated this statement with more coughing.

"Now, Miss Webb," Ellie said soothingly, pouring her a glass of water from the jug on the desk, "the Germans aren't coming. That's why our men are over in Europe – to make sure they don't get anywhere close."

Miss Webb harrumphed, but accepted the glass.

"I expect Dr Pritchard is just making sure he's doing everything properly," Ellie continued. "You wouldn't want him to rush such an important job, would you?"

The old lady gave a grunt, which Ellie decided to take as agreement. "I'm sure everything's under control, but I'll just pop in and see if the doctor needs any help."

The young mother was attempting to soothe her squalling baby again and barely looked up, but Mrs Anderson gave Ellie a grateful smile.

Ellie walked down the short corridor and knocked on the door of the main examination room. There was no answer, so after a few seconds she decided to just walk in. Thomas Pritchard was hunched over her father's desk, head in his hands, surrounded by towering mountains of paperwork.

"Dr Pritchard?" Ellie said, hesitantly.

He startled. "Oh! Oh! Hello, Ellie, I'm afraid you've caught me at rather a bad time. Did you want something?" He pushed his glasses, which had slid to the end of his nose, back up the bridge with his index finger.

"No, no, I'm fine, thank you. But I thought maybe you could do with a hand. . ."

"Oh, ah . . . I'm fine really. Well, no, I'm not. I'm struggling to understand your father's filing system. I can't find anyone's notes." Now he pulled his glasses off altogether and rubbed at them distractedly with a handkerchief. "And I'm terrified of prescribing someone the wrong treatment, without having access to all their medical history. But there are so many people out there and they're getting so impatient, and I can't see the wood for the trees. . ."

"I'm sure I can help. Let me see . . . Yes, look, Daddy keeps the files for Endstone separate from those for elsewhere. It's very simple when you know what to look for, but of course you've only arrived recently so it might not be obvious. . ."

Ellie leaned over the desk. Her father's familiar handwriting leaped out at her from the swathes of notes, and her heart squeezed tight. But she fought the feeling. After all her hopeless knitting, here, at last, was somewhere she could be genuinely useful. She had spent countless hours with her father at his surgery. She knew how his brain worked and understood his systems.

"Whose notes are you looking for?" she asked.

"Mrs Jackson's."

"Is that the lady with the baby?"

He nodded.

"Well, she's not from Endstone, so she won't be in that drawer. Father has the files subdivided into some of the bigger villages, like Fleeting and Haverstock, and then this drawer at the bottom is for people who live in the houses outside of town or on farms."

"Ah!" Thomas's face lit up. "She mentioned a farm. Said her husband would be fed up she'd not been there helping him."

Ellie gave a small smile. "There you go, then." She opened the bottom drawer and located the file.

"That's wonderful, Ellie, thank you so much! I should be able to find these other two now."

"You're welcome," Ellie beamed. "Would you . . . would you like me to file those notes away so that you can actually get to your desk?" she asked shyly.

"Would you mind?"

"Not at all."

"You are an absolute marvel!" They smiled at each other.

Ellie swiftly tidied away the papers from the desk and in a few minutes the place was looking much more organized, and Thomas considerably calmer.

Glancing at the clock, she remembered how late she was. Her mother would be furious. Reluctantly, she began to move towards the door, before remembering something.

"Oh, Dr Pritchard. . . ?"

"Please, Ellie, call me Thomas."

"All right . . . Thomas. Just one more thing. Miss Webb. . . She. . . Well, let's just say, she might be one of your most regular visitors."

"Ah, a bit of a hypochondriac, is she?"

Ellie recognized the word her father had used about the old lady. "Yes, she tends to have . . . or at least *think* she has, everything going. Most of the time she just wants someone to talk to. I believe Father usually finds a ten-minute chat and a prescription of some bedrest do the trick."

"That's a very helpful tip, Ellie! I'm most grateful. In fact, I really can't thank you enough. Please do call back whenever you like!"

"I will," Ellie assured him.

As Ellie cycled back towards home, she felt happier than she had in weeks. A broad smile spread across her face and she hummed loudly to herself.

As she approached the turn-off for her house, she saw Jack with a crowd of his friends and her smile grew even wider.

The other boys peeled off as she approached and Jack waved them away with a call of, "See you tomorrow, lads."

"Well, hello, miss," he said, turning to her with a polite expression and a stagey, upper-class accent. "My name's Jack Scott. I don't believe we've met before."

"Oh, here we go." Ellie giggled as she slowed her bicycle to a stop.

"No, I'm sure I'd recognize you ... Wait! You do look a bit like my old friend, Ellie. But I haven't seen her in a while. She turned into a boring little housewife and forgot all about her old mate Jack."

"Stop it!" Ellie protested. "Any time you want to come round, you're more than welcome!"

"Says you! I'm not sure your mam agrees."

"Hmm. Anyway, I'm not boring and I'm not a housewife. I've just saved poor Dr Pritchard's bacon!"

She told him about the scene she had found at her father's surgery. She called it a daring rescue and Jack laughed.

"Humph. Well, young Eleanor, you may be quite, quite wild, but at least you have made it possible for Miss Webb to get home and be murdered by the Germans in the comfort of her own bed, rather than in your father's surgery!"

"Jack!" Ellie squealed with laughter. "How do you do that? You sound exactly like her!"

They looked at each other and burst out laughing again. "Anyway," he said, slinging an arm roughly around her shoulders, "you did a good job, whether or not the Germans carry Miss Webb off in the end. Your dad'll be very proud when he hears."

Ellie smiled happily at him, contentment spreading through her like a hot cup of tea warming every inch of her.

Seven

Saying goodbye to Jack at the garden gate, Ellie felt her spirits dampen once more. By now she was desperately late.

Leaning her bicycle against the wall, she prepared her defence. Her father had told them to help Thomas. Perhaps she should tell a small white lie and say that someone at school had mentioned that the young doctor was struggling. But Mother already had a low opinion of him; she didn't want to risk making things worse for him. . .

"Is that you, Eleanor?"

Ellie dropped her school bag at the foot of the stairs. "Yes, Mother, it's me. I'm sorry I'm late—"

"Come in here to speak to me, Ellie. Don't bellow from the hallway."

Ellie? Her mother rarely called her by anything other than her full name. As she walked into the kitchen she suddenly became aware of the delicious smell of cooking fish.

Her mother turned round from the oven, an apron tied about her waist. Ellie stared. It was a sight she hadn't seen in months. What had happened?

"Well, now, there you are. Come along, come along, supper is ready. You'd better wash your hands."

Charlie was already seated at the kitchen table, humming quietly to himself, his sandy hair neatly combed.

"Yes, Mother." Ellie moved to the sink as though she were sleepwalking.

"Goodness me, what's the matter with you? Are you unwell?" Her mother marched over briskly and laid a cool hand against Ellie's forehead. Ellie's eyes widened further.

"No, I'm quite well, Mother."

"Well, then, hurry up and get to the table while this fish is still warm."

As the three of them sat at the table together, Charlie chasing his boiled potatoes around his plate with his fingers, Ellie watched her mother curiously. She had barely been out of bed for weeks but here she was, having cooked a proper supper, looking rested and *calm*.

Feeling her daughter's gaze upon her, Josephine swallowed a dainty mouthful, patted her mouth delicately with her napkin and raised her eyebrows. "What is it, Ellie?"

"Nothing, Mother. This is very nice, thank you."

Josephine gave a small nod.

"How was your day?" Ellie ventured.

"It was fine, thank you." Her mother paused, cutting a small chunk of fish into even smaller pieces. "We've had a letter from Father."

Ellie's inhalation was so sharp it carried a morsel of fish with it, which caught in her throat, causing her to splutter in a way that made her mother frown. When she was able to speak again, she gasped, "What does he say? Is he well? May I read it?"

"His regiment has arrived safely in France. He is quite well." Her mother gave a small smile.

"What else does he say?" Ellie's cutlery lay abandoned, a pea rolling slowly away from her fork.

"You may read it for yourself, *after* supper."

"But, Mother—"

"No buts, Eleanor, you know the rules." Josephine's tone had a familiar steely edge to it.

"Yes, Mother."

Ellie ate the rest of her supper as quickly as she could, despite being told twice not to bolt her food. She could feel the fish and potatoes sitting uncomfortably in her upper stomach. She smiled at her mother.

"Please may I be excused?"

Josephine sighed. "All right, then. But you will clear away the supper things once you've finished. I'll bathe Charlie."

"Yes, of course. Thank you, Mother."

Ellie seized the envelope and ran up the stairs to her bedroom. Closing the door behind her, she curled up on her bed, wrapping her body around the letter as though it were a newborn kitten and she its mother.

For the second time that day, the sight of her father's familiar sloping hand brought a lump to her throat that had nothing to do with the poorly chewed supper. She held the envelope to her nose, but there was no trace of her father's smell. She tried to imagine its journey to her as she looked at the strange French stamp.

At last, she opened the envelope and drew out the letter.

1st September 1914

Dearest Josephine, Ellie and Charlie,

Well, we have arrived at last in France after completing our training in Aldershot. The weather here is even lovelier than it was at home this summer, but for me there is nothing in the world so beautiful as the English seaside. Has the weather continued to be fine? The farmers and fishermen had such a marvellous summer!

The journey to France was an adventure in itself. We travelled to Portsmouth by train and from there by boat to France. Some of the Cockney boys didn't know what to do with themselves, having never travelled by boat before. I spent a great deal of the journey ministering to seasick soldiers!

Once we arrived in France, we were put on trucks. Then it was a long march through the cornfields, with French farmers watching us curiously as we passed.

I have been billeted with a splendid group of chaps – we are friends already – and the mood is good. Young Will Scott was sent elsewhere, but I trust he has found himself with equally good men. Perhaps Jack might have heard more – assuming he didn't stow away with a regiment himself!

How are you all? I think of you constantly and miss you dreadfully. I expect Ellie will be back at school by the time you receive this – I hope you're working hard, old girl.

How is Thomas coping? And all my patients? Don't forget to call in when you can and see if Thomas is managing all right. I'm sure he'd appreciate the support.

I'll write again as soon as I can. Until then you'll be in my thoughts and prayers, as always.

All my love,
Wesley (Daddy)

As she read, Ellie felt warmth seeping into her bones as though she were sitting in a hot bath after a chilly winter walk. She wished he had given more detail of where he was, and what his days consisted of, but she'd overheard a girl from school talking about a letter from her own father that had been similarly short on details.

"They're not allowed to write about where they are, you see," she'd said, "in case the letter falls into enemy hands and gives away valuable information."

Ellie dearly wanted to picture where her father was and what he was doing. Still, for those precious moments she felt almost as though he were here in the room with her. Smiling happily and burrowing deeper into her pillow, she prepared to read the letter again from the start.

Eight

Ellie finished the last of the washing up and heaved a sigh. She felt exhausted. After church, she had made Sunday lunch on her own while her mother went to lie down. Charlie had a cold and had been snuffly and crotchety, tugging at her legs and whining for attention while she was trying to cook.

It was a few weeks since they had received the letter from her father and Ellie had felt herself missing him more than ever, and worrying more with every day that passed at the lack of further news. Perhaps her mother was feeling the same, for she had withdrawn back into herself, becoming cold and irritable. She had been giving Ellie an ever-greater number of chores, and these, on top of school and calling into the surgery whenever she could, had left Ellie feeling wrung out like the dish rag she now draped over the stove to dry.

Lifting the kettle from the stove, she poured boiling water into a pot, and waited for the tealeaves to steep. She put the pot on to a tray with a cup and saucer, a small jug of milk and a spoon. Then she carried the tray into the living room, where her mother was sitting in her rocking chair, turning the pages of her Bible without seeming to see them.

"What's this?" she asked as Ellie laid the tray on the small table beside her.

"I thought you might like some tea."

"It's not tea time."

"No, but you were feeling cold earlier. A cup of tea might warm you up."

"Yes . . . well . . . thank you."

"Mother. . ."

"Yes," her mother replied, narrowing her eyes.

"I heard someone mention blackberries at church this morning. It's just the right time of year for them and I thought if I picked enough we could have jam."

"It's Sunday, Eleanor. You're not supposed to be scampering about the countryside."

"I know, Mother, but I promise I won't . . . scamper. And Charlie is asleep so he won't bother you. . ."

"Hmm. . ."

"Please, Mother? Charlie loves jam. It would be such a nice treat for him."

"Well, all right. But you must be home by tea time."

"Yes, Mother. I will!"

Ellie darted from the room before her mother could change her mind. She grabbed a basket and threw an old cardigan on top of her dress.

Jack was waiting at the end of the lane, his usual broad grin on his face. Ellie felt her mood lighten at once. They had managed a whispered conversation after church, and Ellie had promised to see if she could escape for the afternoon. She had only half-expected her mother to agree.

It was a crisp, sunny day, with the first autumn colours showing in the trees and hedgerows. When they reached the corner of the square, Jack tugged the green ribbon from Ellie's hair and ran off with it, making her chase him across the square, down the path and all the way to where the woods began. They were both panting and laughing as he handed it back.

"Good to see you with colour in your cheeks for a change." He grinned, giving her a playful shove.

"It's good to be *out*!" Ellie cried, her voice startling a couple of woodpigeons from the trees nearby. She spun around giddily, kicking up piles of fallen leaves as she went.

"You're mad, you are!"

Ellie shoved him back and they tussled their way through the trees, eventually stopping at a sunny clearing, where they slumped with their backs against the same pine.

"Any word from your dad?" Jack asked.

"No," Ellie said, her heart contracting. "Have you heard anything from Will?"

"Last letter was about a week ago. He never gives any details either. I'm sure he's doing it on purpose," Jack grumbled.

"He is! And you know the reason why. It's not to spite you!"

"I suppose not. It just seems so unfair that he's there

and I'm not."

Ellie frowned. She had thought that with a bit of time, not being old enough to join the army would cease to bother Jack. But if anything, he was becoming steadily more obsessed.

"You know, you might be glad in the end that you didn't go!"

Jack snorted. "I doubt it!"

"Well, maybe you don't know as much about it as you think. I heard Miss Smith and Mr Thompson talking at school. The Germans were well-prepared and the war is not going as we all thought it would. They think it might drag on until after Christmas now."

"Well, that's not so bad. More fun for them!"

Jack was still grinning but Ellie could feel her temper rising. "Fun! It's not fun, Jack! It's men shooting at each other. Killing each other! Have you not even heard about that battle by some river or other in France?"

"Yes, I have, as a matter of fact." Spots of red appeared in Jack's cheeks. "Marne, it's called. And it was a victory for the allies!"

"But at what cost? Mr Thompson said thousands of men were killed. Killed! Not to mention those who were injured."

"That's what happens to soldiers, Ellie. That's why what they're doing is so important!"

"Jack, stop it!" Ellie could hear her voice becoming as shrill as her mother's. "It's not just some game! Our fathers and brothers might come back with horrible injuries, or not come back at all. What purpose does that serve?"

She was on her feet now, standing over him, her hands clenched into fists. If she had thought she could beat him into understanding her, she would gladly have done so.

"Ellie. . ." Jack began, his hands raised pacifyingly.

"No, you listen to me for a change!" Ellie shrieked. Her stomach was churning, but some part of her was glad to be able to shout and stamp. "No one *ever* listens to me!"

He was listening to her now, his forehead knotted in concern.

"You're just like little George, banging away on your tambourine, thinking it's all such good fun. It's easy for you to say, your father isn't out there, risking his life, is he? If war is so very noble, why is he still in The Dog and Duck every night, far from danger?"

Jack winced as though she had hit him in the gut. Ellie felt a corresponding pain in her own chest, but she couldn't have stopped now, even if she had wanted to. "It's not as if he has stayed at home to look after his family. Everyone knows he's a terrible father. It's you and your mother bringing in the money. And now Anna. . . " Ellie scowled. She considered it a dreadful shame that bright Anna Scott had to drop out of school. "We all know everything your father earns he drinks away. . ."

"That's enough, Ellie," Jack said quietly, staggering to his feet.

Ellie paused for a moment, breathing heavily. In the silence her words seemed to echo over and over again in her ears. She swung round and ran from the forest, before Jack could see her cry.

She ran all the way home, stumbling and landing on her ankle more than once, her eyes blurry with tears.

As she approached her front door, she roughly

wiped her face with her handkerchief. But it wasn't enough, not by a long way.

"What on earth have you been doing, Eleanor?" her mother exclaimed as she walked in.

"I *told* you, blackberrying."

"Don't you dare take that tone with me! Look at the state of you! You're filthy! Your hair is full of brambles and your shoes are all scuffed! You're a disgrace."

Ellie gritted her teeth but didn't reply.

"And where are these famous blackberries I was promised?"

Ellie looked around as though the basket might appear, but of course, she'd left it in the woods. It had scarcely had any berries in anyway.

"Nothing to say for yourself? I tell you, Eleanor, I've had quite enough of this behaviour. I scarcely need it on top of everything else I'm trying to cope with. You were with that boy, I presume?"

Ellie didn't answer. She didn't want to think about Jack.

"I thought so and I will not permit it. You are no longer children. It is unseemly. You can wash the windows and floors as punishment, and I suggest you keep out of my sight for the rest of the day if you don't want to make your situation worse."

Ellie turned to the door, feeling her anger draining away into a deep, tired sadness.

Father, she begged in her head. *Please come home! Please let us know you're all right.*

Nine

"Ellie!"

Ellie lifted her head, which had been slumped over her latest knitting attempt – the first one had not been deemed good enough to be sent with the school's package to the troops. This murky green mess looked unlikely to make the cut either.

"I've called you three times already," Miss Smith sighed.

Ellie noticed Rosemary and Janet elbowing each other and giggling.

"Sorry, miss."

She had been finding it harder than ever to focus these past few days. It had been bad enough missing her father, but now she didn't even have Jack. She hadn't heard anything from him since their argument in the woods.

Miss Smith looked at her with a mixture of frustration and sympathy. "Well, come up here and let me see if I can salvage that. And please try to pay attention this time!"

Ellie trudged up to Miss Smith's desk and watched her wrangle with the knotted wool, muttering under her breath.

Ellie's toes curled whenever she remembered the things she'd said about Jack's father. They were unforgivable. But whenever she'd thought about sneaking out to his house to apologize (Josephine didn't approve of her visiting the side of the village where the factory-workers lived), she felt a fresh wave of anger. She was sick of Jack acting as though war was just a game, oblivious to how lonely and terrified she was.

"There now. That'll have to do," Miss Smith said, handing her back the knitting, which had been stripped all the way back to the second row again.

"Thank you, miss," Ellie said distractedly as she returned to her desk.

Maybe her mother had been right all along, she

thought sadly. Maybe she and Jack were from too worlds that were too different. Perhaps now they were growing up it was to hard to ignore.

Miss Smith looked at the clock. "All right, girls, that will do for today. Keep your knitting in your desk and we'll carry on tomorrow."

Ellie groaned softly to herself as she lifted the desk lid and unceremoniously stuffed her knitting into the drawer. As she gathered her things, she heard a sharp ripple of conversation that suddenly stopped as she closed the lid and looked up. Immediately she saw why. Standing before her, with her hands on her hips, was Jack's sister, Anna. Anna had only returned to school for a week after the summer holidays, before dropping out for good. It was common knowledge that she'd had a scholarship, which was why she'd stayed on as long as she had. But her earnings were now needed to support her family; Mabel and Jack's wages just didn't stretch far enough, and Joe's never seemed to make it home from the pub.

"You've got a nerve, Ellie Phillips!" Anna's fists, clenched against her hips, were so tight that her knuckles showed white.

"What—"

"Just like your father, you are. Sticking your beak into things that don't concern you!"

"I don't understand. . ."

Anna was smaller than Ellie, but that made her no less formidable. Ellie looked around, but Miss Smith was in the neighbouring classroom, talking to Mr Thompson. The few girls who were left in the classroom were looking on curiously.

"What business is it of yours if I drop out of school? Where is the shame in working to feed your own family? We can't all be as lucky as you, Lady Muck! Some of us have never had a maid, however hard-done-by you must feel now you've lost yours."

Ellie wanted to speak but instead the words stuck in her throat and she felt choked. Most of the girls had drifted out by now, some looking awkwardly over their shoulders as they went, but one or two had hung back, clearly still enjoying the entertainment.

"And another thing! You can stay away from our Jack; He's a good person; he doesn't need the likes of you—"

"What's going on in here?" Miss Smith was back. "Oh, hello, Anna. It's good to see you again. Is everything all right?"

"Fine, thanks, miss," Anna replied with a tight smile. "Just delivering a message for my mam. Best be off back to the shop."

She stormed out without so much as a glance in Ellie's direction.

"Well, you've certainly managed to tick her off!" Rosemary remarked.

Ellie felt tears starting to fill her eyes once again. She was not normally much of a crier, but these days she was rarely dry-eyed. Grabbing her bag, she ran from the room and into the yard, where she threw herself on to her bicycle and pedalled with all her might. The slow pounding of blood in her ears almost seemed to drown out the creaking of the wheels and the crashing of the waves along the seafront.

She couldn't believe Jack had spoken to Anna about their argument – had told her what she'd said! Her stomach rolled and for a moment she thought she would be sick. Surely Jack knew that she didn't mean it – at least, not the way it had come out? Now Anna hated her and maybe Jack did too. Maybe she deserved it.

That Saturday afternoon, Ellie played cards with her mother in the living room while Charlie happily marched his toy soldiers at their feet. It was rare that Josephine was willing to participate in a shared activity such as this, let alone suggest it, but as Ellie had brought Charlie downstairs after his nap, her mother had all but pounced on her.

"You've been moping around for days now – weeks! Whatever it is, dwelling on it won't help. I always find the best thing is to keep busy."

Ellie thought bitterly of her mother's many hours spent shut away in a darkened bedroom, but she kept quiet. It was an unfamiliar but not unpleasant experience for her mother to be taking an interest. She would not be the one to ruin it.

And in a way, her mother was right. The game was a distraction from the many thoughts running through her mind, even if Mother didn't seem to feel the need for much conversation.

A sudden hammering at the front door startled

them. Mother and daughter looked at each other in surprise for a moment, before Ellie leapt to her feet.

Opening the front door, she saw Jack. The familiar warm feeling spread through her before she noticed his distraught expression.

"Jack—"

"Oh, Ellie, please help. You've got to! It's my dad; he's hurt! I went by your dad's surgery but the sign on the door says the doctor's out visiting a patient."

"What's wrong with your father?" came her mother's crisp voice from the hall. Ellie hadn't even heard her approach.

"He got into a terrible fight at the pub—"

Ellie could hear the sneer in her mother's voice. "Oh? I'm terribly sorry, Jack, but we really can't get involved every time your father's had one beer too many. There would be no end of it! Now, you'll just have to—"

Ellie was unable to listen to another word. Couldn't her mother see how upset Jack was? How scared? She barged past her mother and seized the spare keys to the surgery from the hook in the hallway, tore back out of the door and took hold of Jack's arm.

"Where on earth do you think you're going, Eleanor?"

Ellie didn't even look back. "I'm going to help. That's what Father would do. And it's what he'd want us to do as well."

Ignoring her mother's shouts, she leaped on to her bicycle, and they pedalled away, not exchanging a word until they reached The Dog and Duck. Joe was slumped over his knees on the curb, his hands covering his face. Ted Townsend, a young fisherman, was sitting next to him holding a glass of water and looking as though he'd rather be anywhere else. Ellie could smell the beer on Joe's breath and clothes.

"Thanks, Ted," Jack said, crouching next to his father and resting a hand on his shoulder.

As Joe looked up, Ellie couldn't help but gasp at the sight of his swollen eye and the blood gushing from his nose. His handkerchief was already soaked through. His gaze was unfocused as he turned to his son.

"Jack. . ." He trailed off.

"It's all right, Dad. Ellie's going to let us into the surgery. I'm sure that new doctor will be back soon and he'll have you right as rain in no time."

"Do you think you can walk, Mr Scott?" Ellie asked.

Joe looked up at her without any sign of recognition.

"Come on, Dad, you can walk, can't you?" Jack coaxed.

But Ellie could see that Joe was holding his left arm tucked in protectively against his ribs, and when Jack heaved him to his feet, he staggered and looked as though he would topple over. Ellie couldn't tell if it was his injuries or the alcohol that was making him so unsteady on his feet.

"Give us a hand, eh, Ted?"

Ted and Jack each took one of Joe's arms – he flinched when Jack took his left – and together the four trudged towards the surgery.

Ellie rushed ahead to unlock the door, before leading the men into the examination room. She sent Ted away, and filled a bowl with warm water to wash Joe's face.

Thomas arrived only moments later, as she was gently moving the flannel over Joe's injuries. He sent Jack and Ellie out to the waiting room while he checked Joe over. They sat in anxious silence, but they didn't have long to wait. After a couple of minutes Thomas came out.

"Not much to worry about, Jack, nothing's broken. He's pretty bruised all over and that will hurt when he . . . ah . . . sobers up. He's nodded off in there and I think a bit of a snooze is probably the best thing for him. I'm going to take advantage of it to clean him up a bit more!"

"Thank you, doctor," Jack croaked.

"Not at all, that's my job." Thomas smiled, then returned to the examination room.

"Seems like a decent chap," Jack observed after a few moments' silence.

"He is," Ellie agreed, then paused. "Jack . . . what happened?"

"I don't know for sure. I think it might have something to do with. . ."

He seemed unsure how to continue. Ellie rubbed his arm reassuringly. "Go on."

"Well, Dad and I were in the butcher's earlier – Mam had asked us to pick something up. While we were queuing, this woman comes up to Dad and hands him. . . She passes him a white feather. . ."

"Oh!"

"You know. . . ?"

"I know," Ellie said quickly.

They had been hearing more and more, in the papers and from local gossip, about these white feathers, given by women to able-bodied men who hadn't signed up for the army. The feather represented cowardice. As far as Ellie knew, this was the first one to have been given in Endstone.

"Who was she – the woman?"

"I don't know. She was gone before we properly realized what had happened. But she was no one I recognized. I suppose she might have been one of your Aunt Frances's lot."

"What do you mean?" Ellie didn't understand what this could possibly have to do with Aunt Frances. She was sure her aunt would never be so unkind. Not to mention the fact that she was all the way over in Brighton.

"You know, that Votes for Women crowd seems to be joining forces with the blasted white feather brigade. . ."

They fell silent again, both deep in their own

thoughts. Aunt Frances did talk a lot about the need for women to get the vote, and Ellie knew she had been involved with a group campaigning for this right. But she felt confident her aunt would take no part in humiliating another person, whatever she might think of his actions or politics. It didn't feel the right moment to argue this point with Jack however. She was just glad they were speaking again.

"What happened next. . ." she prompted gently.

"Dad went scarlet and stormed off to The Dog and Duck. I followed, but he told me to leave him alone. It's best not to argue with him when he gets like that, so I did. But he wasn't home a couple of hours later and I was worried. Mam was worried too. So I went to fetch him and found him like you saw. Ted said he didn't see exactly what happened but I reckon maybe someone said something about the feather and Dad just went for them. . ."

"Jack, does he often get into fights?"

"No! He's . . . well, I mean, you know what he's like. He's not what you'd call friendly. But he's not normally violent. It's just that he's been getting more withdrawn since war broke out. He won't talk about it – won't even talk about Will! He pretends none of it's happening. His drinking is getting worse too. . ." He glanced at her, and Ellie tried to keep her face as blank as possible. She didn't want Jack to think she was judging his family again. "It's getting really bad, Ellie. Mam's worried he might lose his job, and then we'll really be stuffed. . ."

Ellie hated to see her friend so worried. She put her hand on his. "It's strange for everyone, Jack. We're all getting used to it. Everything's so different now. But I'm sure things will get better soon. They have to!"

He looked up at her and smiled crookedly. It was a ghost of his usual grin, but a smile nonetheless. "Well, you're the clever one. You're probably right! I don't know why he's so against the war, th—"

He broke off as Thomas re-entered the room, guiding Joe by the elbow. Joe was holding a cold towel to his eye and his gaze was fixed on the floor.

"Like I said, nothing much to worry about. I'm sure you'll be pretty sore for the next few days, not least your head. But there'll be no lasting damage. Erm . . . it might be an idea to lay off the beer for a while, Joe. That won't help your recovery."

Joe and Jack flushed a matching shade of crimson. Ellie knew the embarrassment her friend must be feeling, and her heart went out to him.

"Right, thanks, doctor," Joe muttered, still without looking up. "Come along, lad."

Ellie watched them go, observing how, as soon as he thought they were out of sight, Joe became helpless again, leaning against his son for support.

She thought about Jack. Here she was complaining about all her responsibilities since her father went away, but Jack had been looking after his dad and the rest of his family for years. Everyone thought he was such a joker – Ellie's mother perhaps most of all – but there was a lot more to him than that.

Ten

Ellie glanced anxiously through the window of the village store. She could see Anna talking to her mother. She took a deep breath and puffed out her cheeks. She couldn't avoid Jack's sister for ever. Endstone just wasn't big enough. She pushed against the door with her back, making the bell tinkle as she reversed in with Charlie's pram. She parked him in the corner, cooing happily to himself, and walked up to the counter.

Mrs Scott turned round as she approached and Ellie was shocked by her appearance. She was grey and drawn, and barely managed a smile as she greeted Ellie. "Hello, Ellie, love. How are you?"

"I'm well, thank you, Mrs Scott. How . . . how are you?"

"Oh fine, fine, thank you, my dear," she replied distractedly. "It's nice to see you." She paused and turned to her daughter. "Anna, I just have to bring some more flour through from the back. Will you help Ellie?"

Ellie looked nervously at Anna, but the other girl grinned back at her a little sheepishly, pulling at the end of her braid. Ellie wondered if her helping Jack with their father the other day was responsible for this change. Whatever the reason, she was glad of it. She and Anna had never been especially close, but Ellie didn't like to feel there was animosity between them.

"Hello, Ellie!" Anna said brightly. "What are you after?"

"Just a loaf of bread, please."

Anna reached up to one of the shelves behind her, pulling down a floury loaf and putting it into a paper bag. "How are things at school? I miss it, you know." The admission felt like a small peace-offering to Ellie.

"Do you?" Ellie grinned back. "I'm sick of the place! We're still knitting."

"Oh dear, any improvement?"

"I'm afraid not. I thought I'd try a pair of gloves,

and they seemed to be going well until I got to the end and realized they were both completely different sizes. I think Charlie's probably a better knitter than me!"

"I don't doubt it!" The girls both laughed and Charlie joined in, without the slightest understanding why, which only made them laugh harder. Ellie felt herself relaxing.

Mabel returned from the storeroom and, at the same time, the bell jangled again as Mrs Baxter and Mrs Dorling – widowed sisters both in their seventies – marched in purposefully.

"Good afternoon, ladies," Mabel said. "What can I get for you?"

"Oh, my dear," began Mrs Baxter, "we came to see if you'd heard the terrible news?"

"Terrible!" echoed Mrs Dorling.

"What's happened?" Ellie asked.

"Well, it's poor Billie Farrow," Mrs Baxter went on, shaking her head.

"Just terrible," her sister agreed.

"What about him?" Anna snapped impatiently, earning a scowl from her mother.

"Killed, my dear! Killed in action! His family received the telegram this afternoon."

"They did," Mrs Dorling confirmed.

Ellie felt as though she'd been punched in the gut. A glance at Mabel and Anna suggested they felt the same way. She thought of Billie giving up his Saturdays to coach the Endstone boy's football team, and how much the young lads all loved him. She thought of him laughing outside The Dog and Duck with his best friend Stephen Chase. She thought of him calling out to his fiancée Molly that he'd be back for a Christmas wedding. Poor Molly.

"That's awful. . ." she managed.

"Indeed it is, indeed it is. I had it from Miss Webb and Ethel heard it from Mr Berry in the post office, didn't you, dear?"

"I did."

"Did Mr Berry tell you what had happened to the him?" Ellie asked.

Looking glad to have finally been given the floor, Mrs Dorling tutted. "No, of course not. The telegrams just say 'sympathy and regret' from the army council, that sort of thing. But it's a terrible shame."

"It's a tragedy!"

"It is."

"I just hope no more of our lads follow behind him."

"Indeed. But they've had so little training, especially the young ones. And it seems the Germans are much better soldiers than we were led to believe."

"Quite so, my dear."

"Excuse me, ladies," an ashen Mrs Scott gasped, stumbling out from behind the counter. "I must just go and—" She staggered from the shop without finishing her sentence. Ellie watched her go knowing she was thinking of Will. Anna looked equally shaken. Ellie took a deep breath.

Suddenly the fact that she hadn't heard from her father seemed ten times worse. If only the two sisters would stop wittering on!

"Mrs Baxter!" Ellie exclaimed, causing the two ladies to look round in alarm. "Mrs Dorling! Would you . . . erm . . . would you like to see Charlie's new socks?"

The ladies looked taken aback for a moment, but then bent over the pram. "Well, they're very nice, dear," said Mrs Baxter hesitantly. "Did you make them?"

"Oh, no." Ellie laughed, perhaps a little too gaily, for the sisters looked startled once more. "No, I'm a hopeless knitter, as Anna will tell you. No, my Aunt Frances sent them from Brighton."

"Oh, yes, of course," said Mrs Baxter. "They're a lovely shade of yellow, aren't they, Ethel?"

Charlie chose this moment to pull one of the socks from his foot and throw it to the floor.

"Lovely," Mrs Dorling agreed, puffing a little as she stooped to pick it up. "You know, I always say yellow is so cheering. . ."

Anna gave Ellie a grateful smile but both girls could see that the other was shaken. As Mrs Baxter and Mrs Dorling cooed over Charlie, Ellie thought of her father.

Please, she said silently, without really knowing who she was speaking to. *Please let him be safe. Please let him come home.*

She couldn't bear this feeling of powerlessness. When she managed to drag her mind away from her father it drifted to Billie's fiancée, Molly. Who had told her the news? One of Billie's family, she supposed.

What must she be feeling now? Ellie's mind recoiled from the thought.

When the sisters had finally collected their groceries and left the shop, Ellie bid Anna goodbye and set off once again with the pram.

I want to do something.

Before she was even aware of her intention, she found herself steering the pram towards her father's surgery.

And why not? she thought. It had made her feel better to be useful there before; maybe it would again today.

But when she reached the surgery, it was closed up and dark. There was no sign of Thomas.

With nowhere else to go, she turned the pram up the lane towards home. Charlie began to grizzle and grumble, and distractedly she soothed him, but her mind was elsewhere.

Reversing through the front door with a bump, Ellie stowed the pram under the stairs and released a complaining Charlie to toddle away towards his toys.

Pushing open the kitchen door with a slam, she startled her mother and Thomas, whose heads were bent over some paperwork on the table, cups of tea in their hands.

"Sorry," she said in surprise.

"Oh, there you are," her mother responded. "We were just looking over the surgery's finances."

Thomas, usually so shy and nervous – especially around Josephine – was smiling. Even her mother looked animated and bright-eyed. It was so rare to see her mother comfortable in company that Ellie was momentarily dumbfounded.

"Oh, that's . . . good."

"How are you, Ellie?" Thomas asked warmly.

"I'm. . ." The memory came crashing back and it took her a moment to regain her voice. "Did you hear about Billie Farrow?"

"What about him?" her mother asked.

"He was . . . killed. In action."

Mother's hand went to her mouth.

"That's terrible," said Thomas, all trace of his smile gone. Ellie nodded. He sighed. "The poor man. No wonder they have been asking for more men to sign up. The number of casualties. . ." He stopped, his gaze falling to his teacup.

Silence fell over the room. The cheer that had greeted Ellie evaporated.

"I should call in to the Farrows," Thomas said at last. "Offer my condolences and see if I can be of any assistance to them, or to Miss Fletchling."

Ellie closed her eyes tight, thinking of these people she had known all her life. How could their lives ever be the same again?

In her room later that evening, Ellie sat in front of a blank sheet of paper and sucked on the end of her pen. She must have started a hundred letters to her father but none had made it past the first paragraph. Now it suddenly felt urgent.

Dear Father,

We miss you a lot but we're very proud of you for what you are doing, and there's no need to worry about us. We are all just fine.

I am working hard at school, though I'm sorry to say there is no improvement in my knitting. If only we were given exams in daydreaming – I would be top of the class every time!

Charlie is happy and as funny as ever. I think he's grown since you left. I'm getting big muscles in my arms from lifting him!

Dr Pritchard seems to be doing well and managing fine on his own. I have been into the surgery to help him a few times and gave him a few pointers on your unique filing system – and on Miss Webb's "condition"! Mother and he have been looking at the paperwork and seem to have everything well under control.

I am helping Mother around the house a lot and haven't broken too many plates! I am getting very good at making pies.

The weather is cooling somewhat and there are thousands of blackberries in the woods. Charlie's favourite game is to make his face purple and his tummy gurgle by eating as many as he can before Mother and I realize what he is up to.

I wonder what the countryside is like in France. Do they have blackberries there? Is it warmer than here? I think of you all the time and wonder what you are doing. I know you can't say much about where you are but please tell me a little more next *time you write. I'd like to be able to imagine it.*

When are you coming home, Father? Please let it be soon.

All my love,

Ellie xx

Eleven

A towering pile of logs sat in the centre of the square, interwoven with twigs and bits of old newspaper for kindling. Dr Pritchard and Ted Townsend circled the pile, lighting scraps of paper to try to get the fire going.

The night was crisp, cloudless and beautifully starry. Ellie hugged Charlie closer, as much for her own warmth as for his. Almost the whole village had turned out for Bonfire Night, though not, of course, her mother, who was disapproving of the entire thing – but luckily not so much so that she prevented Ellie from going with Charlie.

Her little brother was squirming in her arms so she put him down. As soon as his feet hit the cobbles, he sped off, as fast as he could on his little legs, in the direction of a crowd of bigger children. Ellie picked up one of his mittens from where it had fallen and hurried after him.

Jack was in the centre of the gathering, playing his fiddle to the delight of Mrs Baxter, Mrs Dorling and other older ladies of Endstone. Around them was the group of whirling, shrieking children. Jack's little brother George stood next to him, beaming proudly, and now Charlie halted next to George, gazing up at the older boy with the same look of awe. Ellie smiled to herself. *Boys.* Always such admiration for the next boy, who might barely be bigger than themselves.

A ragged cheer went up as the fire finally caught and soon the flames were licking up the sides of the pile, sending warm light flickering over the faces of the onlookers and the smell of smoke and burning wood out into the square. Ellie longed to inch closer to the heat but didn't dare move away from Charlie, who was running around at the edge of the crowd, in danger of being trampled by one of the older children.

"Here you go now, my love." Ellie looked round to see Mrs Scott approaching with a steaming flask and a fistful of cups. "You look like you could do with a drop of something to warm those cockles!"

"Oh, thank you," Ellie said gratefully, taking a cup and instantly feeling the heat spread through her gloved fingers. Her mind drifted to France. She wondered how cold it was there, and whether the soldiers had somewhere warm to sleep at night.

A group of children had made a Guy Fawkes and had been taking it from door to door, collecting money. Ellie saw them staggering under its weight as they lugged it towards the flames. They had dressed it in scruffy old khaki-coloured clothes, and put a colander on its head with a stick poking out of the top.

"Burn the Hun!" cried Harry Parkes. "Burn the Kaiser!"

His cry was taken up by some of the other villagers. Ellie frowned. She couldn't put her finger on what it was that bothered her.

The children stopped a couple of yards from the fire. They began to swing the Guy back and forth between them to gather momentum, before releasing it to sail towards the top of the pile, where it dislodged some burning logs, and finally came to rest, quickly catching light. The flames flared higher and an unpleasant, mouldy sort of smell mixed with the scent of burning wood

"You know, if a German soldier were to walk through this square," Mrs Scott whispered to Ellie, "something tells me he would struggle to mistake that chap for one of his countrymen."

Ellie giggled, glad to be distracted from her thoughts. She glanced at Jack's mother, glad she was smiling tonight.

Over Mrs Scott's shoulder, at the edge of the crowd, Ellie saw Molly Fletchling standing with Billie Farrow's younger sister Aggie. In the weeks since the news of Billie's death, his family and fiancée had scarcely been seen around the village, though the Farrows had appeared all three Sundays at church. The first time, Ellie had gone up to them after the service, palms moist and heart pounding so loud in her ears that she could hardly form a coherent thought.

"Mrs Farrow, Mr Farrow," she had choked out, feeling young and stupid. "I am so, so sorry to hear about Billie. We all are. So sorry. . ."

It felt feeble and inadequate. All Ellie could think about was her father convincing Billie to join up, but Bessie Farrow had smiled at her and seized her hand.

"Thank you, Ellie, dear. That's so kind of you."

"Oh, no. . ." Ellie began in protest.

"Everyone's been so kind, haven't they, Mr Farrow?" Her grip on Ellie's hand had got tighter until she almost couldn't feel it any more.

Mr Farrow's eyes were dry but his expression was fierce. "No more than our boy deserved, Bessie. He was the pride of this village!" He looked at Ellie as though challenging her to disagree.

"He was. . ." she started.

"He *was* a good boy," Bessie interrupted, her voice wavering. "I know pride is a sin, but I don't mind telling you, Ellie, I was that proud of him. . ."

Ellie hadn't known what to say. There was nothing to say. She had just stood, holding the woman's hand, until another sympathetic villager had descended, bustling her out of the way.

Molly, on the other hand, hadn't appeared at church. Ellie couldn't remember when she had last seen her. Her heart felt heavy at the thought that it might have been the day when they waved the motorbus off. Molly had been so happy, so sure her Billie would be home for their Christmas wedding.

115

Ellie caught the older girl's eye across the wafting smoke and waved.

I'm sure she doesn't want me to go over, she told herself as Molly half raised her hand in reply. Or was she just being a coward not going to speak to her?

"George, watch *out,*" Mrs Scott called suddenly, interrupting Ellie's thoughts. "Little Charlie is just behind you!"

George looked back impatiently to see Charlie's small but sturdy form wobbling after him. Charlie looked unfazed, smiling gummily at George, who scowled back.

"Don't worry, Mrs Scott, I think Charlie is having the time of his life!"

The sound of her little brother's gurgly laugh was contagious and soon both she and Mrs Scott were laughing too. But Ellie could hear in the woman's voice the same note of desperation that she felt herself, the same threat that laughter might suddenly change to tears. Ellie glanced again at the older woman's face, which looked thinner every time she saw her. She considered asking if she'd heard from Will recently, but decided against it.

Ellie stopped asking her mother if there was any word from her father. It was weeks and weeks since they'd had news – almost a month since she'd sent her own letter. She knew her mother had been writing too. It was unspoken between them, but Ellie knew that her mother was feeling the silence more and more by the day.

The sight of portly Mr Berry the postman walking up the front path earlier in the week had caused her heart to lurch towards her throat. But it had turned out to be a letter from Aunt Frances, who was being sent away for training as a volunteer nurse, having given up her job at the bank.

Once she'd got over her disappointment, Ellie had been delighted to hear from her aunt and very excited to learn about her volunteer work. But she knew better than to discuss it with her mother, who cast only the briefest eye over the letter, one eyebrow arched and lips pursed tightly.

A tug at her leg drew Ellie's attention back to the present. She looked down to see a sleepy Charlie, his arm wrapped behind her knee and his woollen hat knocked to one side.

"Come on then, you," she said, reaching down to heave him into her arms.

His cheeks were pink and his eyelids heavy as he rested his head against her shoulder, one thumb creeping towards his mouth.

Feeling him still and secure in her arms, Ellie at last moved closer to the fire, rocking him as she went. The crackling hiss of the burning logs felt almost hypnotic. Her eyes were mesmerized by the dancing flames that engulfed the blackened remnants of the Guy, as the notes from Jack's fiddle soared up towards the smoke-filled sky.

Twelve

Ellie woke, feeling toasty under her blanket, and stretched carefully, trying to avoid any part of her meeting the cold air outside the bed before it absolutely had to. Perhaps as a result of all the fresh air, she had slept better that night than she had done for weeks, too exhausted from the festivities to let the usual worries rattle through her brain and keep her awake.

Releasing one arm out into the chill of the room to tweak the curtain, she was surprised to see that it was already getting light outside – normally Charlie would have had her awake long before she needed to think about getting up for school. Maybe he'd slept extra deeply too.

Tucking her arm back in, she called to him, "Morning, Charlie boy. Did you have nice dreams about the big fire?"

Silence. None of his usual happy gurgles and coos. Maybe her mother had been in and got him out of his cot already. Ellie wondered why she hadn't woken her too.

Ellie frowned and swung her feet out of bed and into her slippers, inhaling sharply as the cold air hit her skin. She grabbed a cardigan from the back of the chair and shrugged her arms into it.

"Charlie," she called again as she walked over to his cot, but she fell silent as she saw him.

Her brother stared up at her with wide blue eyes, still making no sound. His skin was pale but damp-looking and as she watched she could see him shivering.

"Oh, baby boy, are you not well?" She put a hand to his clammy forehead, sweeping away strands of wet blond hair – it was burning hot. Panic jolted through her. "Don't worry, little lamb, I'll get Mummy." She pulled the blanket from his bed and tucked it around him, before rushing down the hall to their mother's room.

Mother was sitting at her dressing table in her nightgown and dressing gown, washing her face with water from an enamel basin. Her silvery hair was tied back in a tight braid. Catching sight of Ellie's reflection in the mirror, she said, "There you are. You'd better hurry up or you'll be late for school."

"Mother, there's something wrong with Charlie."

Ellie couldn't remember ever seeing her mother move so quickly; she was on her feet before the sound of her daughter's last word had died away, sloshing water from the basin in her haste.

They hurried back to Charlie, who was lying completely still in his cot. Mother felt his temperature with her hand and gasped. "Oh, he's really not well." She lifted him carefully out of the cot and cradled him against her, wrapping the blanket tight about him. Ellie hovered anxiously. "He must have caught a chill. You did dress him properly last night, didn't you?"

"Yes, Mother."

"You didn't forget to put his woollen underclothes on?"

Ellie frowned. "Of course not."

Charlie gave a soft moan and Mother kissed him

121

gently on the top of his head, before turning back to her daughter. "You're always letting him run around without his hat on – was he wearing it last night? It was so cold."

The sight of her little brother shuddering in her mother's arms, set Ellie's stomach churning. "Of course he was, Mother. You know, if you don't trust me to look after him properly, maybe you should do it yourself." The words were out of her mouth before she had time to check them. She braced herself for her mother's reaction, but she seemed scarcely to have heard her.

"Now, Charlie, don't worry," she crooned into his damp hair. "Mummy's here."

"I'll go and get Thomas," Ellie blurted out, desperate to be moving, to be doing something.

Again there was no response from her mother.

"Mother?"

"Yes, go, go," she snapped. "Hurry!"

Ellie seized a skirt and blouse from her wardrobe, before yanking her nightgown over her head and flinging it to the floor. Normally she would have been shy getting changed in front of her mother, but it was the last thing on her mind now. Her mother seemed to be unaware that she was still in the room.

She dressed as quickly as she could and ran from the room, down the stairs and out of the house. She flung herself on to her bicycle and started down the lane, pushing it to its absolute limits, standing on the pedals the whole way to the surgery.

Thomas looked pleased to see her but quickly grasped that it was not a social call. Seizing Ellie's father's bicycle that he was using in his absence, he followed her swiftly back to the house.

Arriving out of breath they threw down their bicycles at the front of the house and ran up the stairs. Ellie could hear her mother's voice coming from her bedroom now.

"What took you so long?" Mother was perched on her bed, holding a damp flannel to Charlie's forehead.

Ellie couldn't have been longer than twenty minutes in total, but she didn't argue. She was embarrassed to see that her mother still wasn't dressed. A glance at Thomas's red face showed that it had not gone unnoticed.

The young doctor moved towards the bed, where

Charlie was lying listlessly, face wan and eyelids flickering.

"Oh, if only Wesley were here!" Josephine moaned. "He would know what to do!"

Thomas flinched. Ellie could almost see his nervousness and uncertainty come flooding back.

"I – I will do everything I can," he stammered.

Mother waved this away with an impatient hand. "You could never replace him! Now, *do* something!"

"Y-y-yes, of course, I – if you could just. . ."

"Mother, he needs you to give him some room so that he can get to Charlie," Ellie burst out in exasperation.

Mother swung round, her hair escaping from its braid in wild tendrils that framed her face. Ellie thought of all the times her mother had told her that she looked wild and felt a startling and entirely inappropriate gurgle of laughter rising in her throat. She swallowed it down and they looked at each other for a long moment before Josephine gave a curt nod and stepped away from the bed.

"Thank you," Thomas breathed. "Ellie, might I trouble you to cool this flannel in some fresh water?"

"Of course." Ellie hurried down the stairs to wet the flannel in the kitchen sink. As she returned to the bedroom a few moments later she could hear her mother. Her voice was ragged with emotion

". . .tried and tried for years after Eleanor. Three. We lost three."

Ellie stopped still in the doorway, scarcely breathing. Her eyes fell to the faded carpet and seemed to become fixed there.

There was a sobbing breath. "Wesley told me that it wasn't going to work, that I was making myself unwell. That Ellie was enough for us and we had to give up. . ." Josephine broke off again.

Ellie stood frozen. She had known about the lost babies – some of them, at least. She had been old enough to know when her mother was expecting a baby – and then suddenly wasn't any more. She had known that Mother had been terribly ill. But she had never heard her speak so openly about it. Even her father didn't speak so openly about it. For her mother to be sharing something so personal with Thomas – someone who until so recently had been a complete stranger. . . Ellie felt her throat go dry.

"I can't lose him, Thomas, I can't," Mother burst out again. "I can't, I can't, I can't. . ."

Thomas looked around at Ellie, his eyes wide in appeal. She rushed forwards, thrust the flannel at him and took hold of her mother's elbow.

"Come on, Mother, let's have a cup of tea downstairs."

"I can't leave him!"

"You must," Ellie replied firmly. "We're in Doctor Pritchard's way here, we're stopping him from doing his job properly."

That seemed to get through. Thomas gave Ellie a grateful look as Mother allowed herself to be led away.

Downstairs, they sat across the kitchen table from each other in silence, their tea untouched. The ticking of the kitchen clock sounded unnaturally loud. Ellie pictured Charlie's flushed cheeks the evening before. He'd seemed so excited, so happy. Should she have been worried? Maybe she ought to have put an extra cardigan on him – it had been very cold. And he had kept pulling off his mittens. Surely that alone couldn't have made him so ill?

After what felt like hours, they heard Thomas's

footsteps on the stairs and lurched to their feet, their chair legs screeching in unison against the kitchen floor.

"He seems stable," the doctor began, without ceremony, "but he's weak and has a fever."

"We didn't need you to tell us that," Mother muttered.

"I can't say for certain what ails him, but I'll keep a close eye on him over the next few days. In the meantime, keep him warm and quiet, and get as much water into him as you can."

"That's it?" Josephine demanded, her voice shrill.

"For now," Thomas replied. "Please trust me. You must be patient. I will be back later today to check on him, but come and get me at once if anything changes."

Thirteen

By the next day, there was no change in Charlie's condition. It was all Ellie could do to force occasional sips of water or tea into her mother – she wouldn't eat anything more, or even leave the bedroom except to visit the outhouse.

Thomas visited twice a day, as promised, and urged Ellie to make thin broths and get her mother and brother to drink as much of them as she could.

"Your mother's nerves are at breaking point, Ellie," Thomas told her gently. "I don't want to alarm you, but you must try to keep her as calm, rested and nourished as possible or she will become unwell."

Ellie had scarcely any appetite either but forced herself to keep eating regular meals; as her mother got weaker, she knew she couldn't afford to fall ill too.

It wasn't long before Mother stopped leaving her bed, and, sure enough, when Ellie checked on them both on the evening of the second day, her mother's forehead felt like a kettle fresh from the stove. She tucked them in together and sat with them as they tossed and turned feverishly.

She waited for a letter from her father with renewed desperation. Surely he would sense that they needed him? Surely he would know that she couldn't cope on her own?

Of course, she couldn't go to school. She was kept busy all day, looking after her mother and Charlie and trying to prevent the house from falling into total squalor. Then the evenings were a slow, quiet torment of loneliness and anxiety. Once all the chores were done, Ellie tried to take her mind off things by reading. But she couldn't focus on her book for long; her feet kept taking her to her parents' room where she would stand in the doorway, watching her mother and Charlie as they slept, observing the laboured rise and fall of their chests.

She couldn't even write to Aunt Frances, who hadn't yet let them know the address of her nursing training facility. Ellie thought of her cheerful, practical aunt with a longing that was almost physical.

By the third day, even Thomas wasn't able to stay long. It had turned colder and more people were ill in Endstone. The war meant many were working harder than ever and without enough to eat. They were even more vulnerable to the infection that seemed to be spreading. The only good thing about this was that it reassured Ellie that she had not been responsible for Charlie's illness, a notion that Thomas too was keen to dispel.

"Ellie, it's a virus. People are getting ill all over the region – all over the country, according to the papers. Even if Charlie did get a bit of a chill that night, it's extremely unlikely that he would have been able to fight off this bug. Small children and the elderly are always the first to succumb to any sort of epidemic."

Ellie couldn't stop herself from dwelling on how different things might have been were her father home. Not only would he have been able to help the patients on a practical level, but he also care for the large numbers of patients, but he would also have provided a valuable link with the rest of the village. Ellie's mother had always been standoffish, but Father was loved by almost everyone. With him gone, they had been receiving fewer and fewer visitors. Now that she was housebound, Ellie realized she had never felt so alone.

Of course, Jack stopped by as often as he could between work and his own family commitments. On the evening of the fifth day after Charlie got sick, he came round, whistling cheerfully as ever and bearing a loaf of bread. The combined effect of his familiar, smiling face and this kind gesture was almost too much for Ellie. She stared fixedly at the table, trying to prevent a tell-tale tear from slipping down her cheek and betraying her.

"Steady on, El. It's only a bit of bread!" Jack clapped a hand on her shoulder and squeezed.

"I know, but it's so kind of your mother." Ellie was all too aware of how little the Scotts had to spare, and the fact that her own mother had never done anything to help them, though she was in a far better position to do so. She remembered Anna's comment about the maid and cringed.

"*Pfft*. You know my mam's got a soft spot for you and your Charlie. Besides, she's ever so grateful to you for helping us out with Dad that time." Jack looked at a point over Ellie's shoulder as he said this last part. "Anyway, did I tell you, we've had a new letter from our Will?"

Ellie winced. Jack didn't seem to notice. *And why would he?* she thought. She hadn't told anyone about how long it was since they'd heard from Father. Voicing her worries would only make them more unbearably real.

"He sounds a changed man," Jack continued, oblivious. "He's thriving. He's been promoted to lance-corporal and everything. It's like I always said, there are opportunities for boys like us out there that we just don't get at home. . ."

As he reported anecdotes and jokes from Will's letter, Ellie felt her stomach twist and curl. She was pleased for Jack and his family, she really was, but why hadn't they heard from Father? There was clearly no issue with letters getting through. . . There must be a good reason. There had to be. She wished she could believe it.

It wasn't long before, feeling disgusted with herself,

she interrupted Jack's account, pleading the need to check on the patients, and bustled him from the house.

The next day she was pleased and surprised when the family's old maid Alice came to visit. It was months since they had had to let her go, but she'd heard in the village about Josephine and Charlie being unwell, and had thought Ellie might need some help. She had brought apples and helped Ellie chop vegetables for a broth, but more than anything, it was her company and her good nature for which Ellie was glad. They had always got on and the maid had sometimes covered for Ellie when she returned late from one of her adventures with Jack.

After about twenty minutes, however, her mother's shrill voice sounded upstairs.

"Is that Alice I hear?"

"Yes, Mother," Ellie called, hastening to her feet, anxious about what might follow.

"What is she doing here?"

"She's—"

"Doesn't she understand that we don't require her services any more?"

Ellie hurried up the dark staircase as fast as she could go, her face burning.

"Show her the door," snapped her mother.

"Mother—"

"It's all right, Ellie." Alice's soft voice interrupted her. "She's not well. Let's not upset her. I'll go."

Ellie turned slowly at the top of the stairs. But it wasn't anger she saw in her old friend's eyes. It was shock. And sympathy. Josephine had always been cool and curt with Alice, but the look on the other girl's face made Ellie realize just how much stranger her mother's behaviour had become. She walked slowly back down towards her.

"Alice—"

"I'm all right, Ellie," she repeated. "But are you?"

No. No, no, no, no.

She forced her mouth into the semblance of a smile. "I'm fine," she insisted brightly, then lowered her voice. "Just a bit tired. And Mother's fever is making her feel a bit peculiar, I think."

Her mother's voice drifted back down. "Is she still here?" Both girls flinched.

"I'd better go," Alice said. "But I'm never far if you need me, remember that, Ellie."

Ellie did not allow her smile to waver until Alice was out of sight. Then she was alone again.

134

Fourteen

Ellie was washing dishes in the kitchen when she saw Mr Berry the postman push open the gate and proceed up the garden path. Charlie and Mother's fevers had finally broken a few days before and Ellie had seen the improvement immediately. They were more alert and each had eaten a few small bowls of broth. As a result, Ellie had managed to get a good night's sleep, and felt rested and more positive, though a heavy atmosphere still hung over the house.

The sight of the postman made her forget everything else but the roaring of blood in her ears. She stood, her hands gripping the edge of the basin so tightly that her knuckles seemed illuminated, watching him make his tortuously slow way towards her.

The postman was oblivious to her gaze until he was standing right in front of the window. He gave a little start, then smiled broadly.

"Ah, good morning, young Ellie." He waved a handful of envelopes.

Ellie left the kitchen and walked to the front door, releasing a juddering breath she hadn't known she was holding.

"Thank you, Mr Berry," she said shakily. She recognized her father's handwriting on all three of the envelopes. She closed the door as soon as she could without seeming rude and raced up the stairs to her mother.

Mother was sitting at her dressing table, washing her face. She was alone. Charlie had returned to his own cot and Ellie to her own bed the night before. Her mother turned as soon as she heard Ellie's hurried footsteps.

The two of them sat perched on the same wide stool and tore their way hungrily through the envelopes. The first couple had been sent weeks earlier and must have been held up somehow. They did not savour the letters this time, as they had with Father's first letter from

France, but hurried through them, stopping only to read aloud the odd snippet and laugh with an abandon that an observer would have thought out of proportion to the jokes and stories being told.

Father was well and sounded in good spirits. Morale was high, he told them, and he'd grown closer to some fine fellows whom he was proud to call friends. He was now working in a medical tent and, while there was far too much work for one person, he was glad to be back doing what he was best at. From what he could tell they were making good progress, though it was taking longer than everyone had hoped to beat the Germans. He would still be home for Christmas, he told them, he was sure of it.

His regiment had adopted a stray dog, which they'd named Patch and who now followed them from place to place. Wesley enclosed a picture he'd done of the dog for Charlie, which wasn't very good, but which nonetheless made Ellie's heart feel as though it were dragging itself deeper into her chest.

As with his previous letter, all three were filled with questions about the family, the surgery and Endstone in general. He sounded delighted that Ellie had been helping out at the surgery and joked that she'd probably be running it by the time he came home. He didn't mention when this would be, but made hopeful references to seeing them soon.

Ellie and her mother exchanged a glance, thinking of how much had happened that he knew nothing about. Ellie wondered what he would say if he knew about Billie Farrow. It did not seem from the letters that the news had reached him.

"I should show Charlie the picture of the dog," Ellie said finally. "He'll love it."

"Oh, yes," Josephine replied, her eyes glistening, "yes, yes."

Before Ellie knew what was happening, her mother had wound an arm around her shoulders and pulled her towards her chest. The room suddenly felt very quiet. Ellie sat unmoving – scarcely breathing – for a moment before, slowly, slowly, she wrapped her own arms around her mother's narrow waist. They sat like this for what felt like the longest time.

All of a sudden, life returned to a kind of normality. It was as though the letters had sped Mother through the final stages of her recovery, and in a few days she was back to full strength and took over nursing Charlie.

Ellie returned at last to school, where she was greeted warmly by Miss Smith, who seemed as worried by her pale, tired appearance as by her prolonged absence. After so long cooped up in the house, Ellie found herself glad to be back at school, in the company of other girls and with other things to think about. The hubbub of conversation was a relief after the quiet at home. Cookery classes seemed more interesting than usual too, now that they were all having to make do with less. Even knitting felt more bearable than before.

As the weeks passed, Ellie called in at the surgery as often as she could, frequently staying for a couple of hours at a time. She would help Thomas with the filing, or else sit with the patients in the waiting room, entertaining them with conversation or card games, and helping frazzled mothers with their children.

Thomas took to calling her "matron" and, though a joke, it gave Ellie a fizz of pride in her chest every time she heard it. That awful fortnight when her mother and Charlie had been so ill had shown her that she had got a certain amount of satisfaction from taking care of people and doing it well. Even the most dull household chores seemed less boring when people were in genuine need. It surprised her to realize how much she'd changed in the last months.

A few days after Father's letters arrived, Ellie returned from school to find her mother wearing an apron and a headscarf, on her hands and knees scrubbing the kitchen floor. Ellie had been fairly sure the house was spotless before she had left that morning, but it was certainly gleaming now.

"Mother, what are you doing? You're still weak; you shouldn't be doing anything strenuous."

Her mother protested, but eventually allowed herself to be sat down at the kitchen table, as Ellie hefted the kettle on to the stove.

"Well, if you're not going to let me finish it, you'd better do it yourself. And then the mantelpiece needs dusting. . ." Her mother's eyes cast wildly about for more imagined grime.

"But, Mother, the place is perfectly clean."

"Well, Eleanor, we all know what your standards are like. I cannot allow things to slip any further around here. We must make sure everything is perfect for when your father returns. It could be any day now."

Silently, Ellie questioned how likely it was that her father would notice the cleanliness of the floor. Aloud, she said, "But he hasn't even told us when he's coming back yet. I'm sure we'll have plenty of warning." Ellie saw her mother's face fall. "But I'll make sure everything's perfect, I promise," she added hastily. "You look exhausted. You don't want to get ill again, do you? Why don't you finish that tea and then have a lie down?"

Her mother looked like she might be ready to argue but then, to Ellie's surprise, she nodded meekly. She clambered painfully up the stairs and Ellie tidied away the tea things, gave the floor a cursory sweep and flicked a duster over the mantelpiece.

Checking on Charlie, she found him dozing, still weak but finally free from fever. She brushed a blond curl back from his face and tucked his teddy in closer to him.

Happy that her mother and brother were sleeping peacefully, Ellie pulled her coat on and set off out of the house, down the path into the village. Her feet crunched over the last of the fallen leaves, sending squirrels scampering back to the shelter of the trees. As she drew closer to the main square, she picked up the sounds of Jack's band of friends playing music, the notes from his fiddle seeming to soar higher and clearer than the rest. She found them outside The Dog and Duck, and sat on a bench nearby, clapping and singing along with the tunes she knew, enjoying being outside with people around her.

After a while, Jack said goodbye to his friends and, slinging his fiddle over his shoulder, came to join her. He suggested a walk around the village, which she happily agreed to, glad to have the chance to be alone with him.

The village was dark, illuminated only by the light spilling from The Dog and Duck and the surrounding houses, and the two electric street lights in the square. These shone warmly on the slight frost that had begun to settle, making it sparkle, and Ellie imagined gemstones twinkling in a dark mine. After a while of comfortable silence, Jack remarked, "Christmas soon."

"Mmm. It feels as though ten years have passed since last Christmas," Ellie replied.

"I feel like it's flown by!" her friend exclaimed.

"Yes, but think about how much has happened since then. This time a year ago, Alice was still working for us. Of course, I could do nothing right for Mother even then, but now. . ." Ellie's voice trailed off. She didn't feel, even with her best friend, that she could admit how strange her mother had become, how worried she was about her behaviour.

Jack glanced sideways at her and moved closer – just a couple of centimetres, but the gesture made her sure of his support.

They had passed the turn-off for the woods, and continued on, in the direction of the station.

Ellie continued, "And there was no war, and your Will was still home. And Father." She swallowed, quickly steering her mind away from the thought of Billie Farrow, who would never be home again. "Father's never really understood the way Mother and I don't get on, and of course he can be strict himself, but . . . I don't know. It was nice to feel I had a friend at home, someone who didn't think I was such a disaster, someone who – just sometimes – was proud of me." Ellie's sudden laugh echoed from the walls of the houses nearby. "And Charlie was only new then, and something we all agreed on was that he was just perfect." Her brow smoothed as she thought of how content they had been to sit staring at the baby for hours on end, entranced by his every move.

"I thought life was hard, then! I had no idea how happy I was!" She laughed again but there was no humour in it, only bitterness.

They drew level with the church now. The candles, visible through the stained glass window at the front, seemed to shimmer and glisten. The vision was almost mesmerizing. So intent was her gaze that she didn't notice Jack take a step towards her and was caught unawares when he grasped her hand and drew her to face him.

"Ellie. . ." His brow was furrowed. His look was one of almost painful concentration. "Ellie, I hope so much you'll be happy like that again. In fact, I feel sure you will be. You . . . you're special. You're different. Life will be happy and exciting for you, just wait and see."

Ellie had never known Jack to speak at such length and with such passion.

"And I'm proud of you, all right? So you never need to think it's just your dad."

The warmth in his words set off an answering glow in her tummy. She smiled at him. "Sorry to be so serious. We hadn't heard from Father for so long, and then there was poor Billie. . . And Charlie and Mother being so sick . . . and I think all that worry has been gnawing away in my brain so that's now full of holes!"

Jack smiled back at her, looking relieved that she hadn't teased him. He gave a little tug on her right hand and took hold of her left too. "Why didn't you tell me, you daft thing? I know I don't always have the right words, and I'm not as clever as you but . . . I don't know. I just don't like to think of you worrying about these things all on your own."

Ellie opened her mouth to reply, but broke off at a sudden volley of kissing sounds, followed by a peal of giggles. They both spun round in time to see George springing like a Jack-in-the-box from behind the moss-covered wall of the churchyard, slipping out of reach of Anna, who was just behind him.

"What are you doing, you little toad?" Jack exclaimed, as his brother hopped over the wall and forced his way between them. "Shouldn't you be at home in bed?" He scowled at his sister Anna.

"Don't look at me like that," she retorted. "I've been chasing him for ages trying to get him back home." But her knowing smirk left Ellie unconvinced as to how hard she'd really been trying, at least since they had arrived by the church.

"I should be heading home myself," Ellie said. She bid goodnight to the Scotts and watched them walk off, George maintaining a stream of commentary about when Jack thought he would "pop the question". But just as she was preparing to set off for home, Ellie saw Jack turn round and give her a smile and a wink. She set off with a skip to her step. Let them laugh; they meant no harm and they could not spoil the moment.

Fifteen

Ellie was clearing away the tea things when Mr Berry arrived with the post. As always when she saw him waddle up the path, she tried to keep her mind perfectly blank, all the while aware of the pounding in her chest and the sensation of her tongue, dry and leaden in her mouth.

But the changing nature of his job meant that Mr Berry, not especially known for his sensitivity and tact, was learning to anticipate how keenly and with what mixed feelings his visits were met. As he closed the gate behind him, he squinted up towards the window and gave Ellie a cheerful wave. Releasing her lower lip from the clamp of her teeth, she hurried to the door to greet him.

"Good afternoon, Ellie!" Mr Berry smiled as she opened the door, handing her a cluster of envelopes.

"Good afternoon, Mr Berry," she replied. She forced herself to ask after his health and his family, her eyes darting all the while to the envelopes – and specifically the one on which she could see her father's handwriting.

When he eventually bid her goodbye, she politely watched him make his way back down the path, before closing the door and whirling round – only to come face to face with her mother.

Before Ellie could say anything, her mother snatched the envelope written in her father's hand and retreated into the kitchen with it, like an animal stealing away with a pilfered treat. Frowning, Ellie followed and took a seat across from her at the table. Her mother read in silence, so Ellie, swallowing her impatience turned her attention to the other items of post.

The first was a Christmas card from one of her father's patients in a neighbouring village; the other a card and letter from Aunt Frances. Ellie read her aunt's news with relish, glad to have something to focus on while she waited for her mother to finish reading.

Frances was now working as a volunteer nurse, looking after wounded soldiers as they returned from the Front. Although she hinted at having seen some terrible things, her letter focused on the funny stories related by the soldiers, how rewarding it was to help them back to health, and how much fun she had with the other nurses, who sounded like a lively and mischievous bunch.

When Ellie eventually looked up, she was surprised to see her mother's head cradled in her hands, the letter lying abandoned beside her. Ellie's frown deepened. It clearly wasn't the worst news – the letter was from Father himself. What, she wondered, could have caused this reaction?

Ellie reached across and pulled the letter towards her. A smile spread across her face as she saw the familiar scrawl spilling across the page. She began to read, closing her eyes briefly, imagining his voice recounting the same story of the sleep-talking soldier from the letter. Opening them again, she skimmed on and then stopped.

There it was, about three quarters of the way through the letter:

*I am so sorry to have to tell you that it seems I
won't be home for Christmas after all. I'm sure
this is disappointing news for you – it certainly is
for me. But at least there will be more of Frances's
Christmas pudding for Charlie boy. If he's still
eating at the rate he was before I left, he must be
twice the size by now! I just hope that enough
of his teeth have come through that he can be
encouraged to chew properly!*

Ellie ran her hand over the dips and ridges his pen had etched into the paper. Christmas had been the focus for so long. . . She blinked back the tears that were forming in her eyes.

Just as she was forcing herself to read the end of the letter, there was a jaunty rap at the door. Mother remained motionless, so Ellie went to answer it.

It was Thomas, calling to check up on them. He gave Ellie a searching look, then launched quickly into a story about Miss Webb's latest visit, only breaking off as he caught sight of Mother's face.

"Whatever is the matter?"

"Oh, Thomas! How much more can I be expected

to bear?" Mother was on her feet now, hands braced against the table.

Thomas moved towards her, his hands outstretched. Mother collapsed against him, sobbing into his chest. He threw Ellie a panicked look as he placed his arms around her.

"We've heard from Father," Ellie explained quietly. Her face felt as though it were burning; she wanted to force her mother away from the doctor and back to her seat. "He won't be home for Christmas after all."

Mother gave a wailing cry that made both Ellie and Thomas flinch.

"Now, now," Thomas said in a firm tone. "You must remain calm. You'll make yourself unwell again. Come along, let's get you upstairs."

As they reached the top of the stairs, Charlie toddled out of the children's room, wearing his pyjamas.

"Mama?" he asked, eyes wide.

"Don't worry about Mama, Charlie. Come to me." Ellie scooped her little brother into her arms and followed Thomas into her mother's room. Thomas helped her mother into bed and took her pulse.

"This won't do, Josephine. I'm worried about you,"

he murmured. "This anxiety. . . Your nerves. . . You do want to be well when Wesley returns, don't you? I know that's what he'd want. It's what I want, what your children want. . ."

His voice was low and soothing. As the sobs subsided, Ellie carried her little brother back down the landing to their room, where she tucked him into his cot.

By the time she'd got him settled and had returned to her parents' bedroom, her mother's eyes were closed and her breathing regular.

Thomas and Ellie went back downstairs and stopped by the door. Ellie didn't know what to say. Her mother's behaviour was stranger by the day.

Thomas broke the silence at last. "Fetch me at any time if you're worried, won't you, Ellie? Day or night."

She nodded.

He put a hand on her shoulder and looked probingly into her eyes. "I am sorry about your father. I'm sure it's a terrible disappointment."

Unable to withstand his gaze, Ellie lowered her eyes. A tear that had been hovering on the brim of her lower eyelid escaped and trickled treacherously down her cheek.

Thomas crooked a finger under her chin and tilted it so that she was looking at him again. "You are a very brave young woman, do you realize that? I see now that it wasn't just fatherly bias causing Wesley to speak so highly of you."

This brought a wobbly smile to Ellie's face.

"You have friends, Ellie, remember that. You don't have to be brave all the time."

Ellie wasn't expecting to see her mother the next morning, but she appeared in the kitchen while Ellie was giving Charlie his breakfast, dressed and looking brighter. She accepted the tea and toast that Ellie put in front of her with a rare smile, and seemed to be in no hurry to re-embark on one of her manic cleaning sessions.

"I have to leave for school in a moment," Ellie said, looking at her mother warily. "But I can stay if you're not well enough to look after Charlie."

"No, no, you must go." Her mother's cheeks flushed pink. "I'm . . . I'm sorry, Eleanor." She busied herself wiping an invisible smudge from Charlie's face. "Thomas is right. I must try to get better. I *will*. He . . . he suggested joining the knitting circle that some of the village women have formed. It's a little silly, I know, but he thinks I'd feel better if I had something positive to focus on, something I could do to help. And I think he could be right."

Ellie understood that feeling all too well, even if there was little she herself would like to do less. "I think it's a wonderful idea!" she declared, beaming at her mother. She had never thought she'd see her mother willingly join a village club.

Mother smiled back, somewhat uncertainly. "Well, I can't just sit at home waiting for your father to come back, can I?"

"You're absolutely right, Mother," Ellie replied decisively. "He would want us all to do whatever we can to help."

"Yes," Mother said softly. "I think he would."

Sixteen

Ellie flung down her book and hurtled into the kitchen, which was thick with the smell of cinnamon and nutmeg. Seizing a tea towel, she opened the oven door and yanked out the tray of mince pies. Just in time. The pastry was golden and flaking, the fruit glistening stickily in the centres.

Leaving the tray on the sideboard, Ellie dug around in the cupboard for the cooling tray, and transferred the pies to it, giving little gasps of pain as the hot pastries burned her fingertips. Her mother would have chided her and told her to wait until they were cooler. But her mother was not at home; it was the evening of her knitting group. She had been going for a few weeks now and, to Ellie's surprise, showed no sign of renouncing her promise to Thomas. She had discovered that the other ladies loved it when she brought Charlie with her. Given that she wasn't exactly adept at these social situations, his presence had soon proven invaluable. He'd become a permanent fixture after the first few sessions and Ellie had been enjoying the time to herself, free from Charlie-minding duties and her mother's supervision.

Ellie yanked the last pie from the tin too roughly and it crumbled in her hand, piping hot pieces of fruit tumbling into her palm. She crammed the whole thing into her mouth, her burned tongue a worthwhile sacrifice for the explosion of sweet and spicy flavours. Licking the last crumbs from her fingers, she surveyed the rack of cooling pies. Jack loved mince pies. He loved most food, but he had an especially sweet tooth. She hadn't seen him for more than a few fleeting moments since their walk round the village back in November. Mother never liked Ellie to visit the Scott house – it was at least a year since she'd been there – but her mother wasn't here, and what she didn't know couldn't hurt her.

Ellie found a basket in the cupboard under the

stairs, lined it with a clean cloth and piled it high with mince pies, before tucking another cloth neatly on top. She, Charlie and Mother would never manage them all anyway, she thought to herself. Wrapping herself up in scarf, hat, gloves, coat and boots, she left the house and hooked the basket over her bicycle handlebars. Then she set off for Jack's house.

The path down to the village was gently sloping, and the frost and icy puddles made it more treacherous. Ellie took the descent slowly. It was only when she got to the square that she began to enjoy skid-sliding across the cobbles.

On the far side of the village from Ellie's home was a grid of terraced streets, in which most of the factory workers lived. King George Street was one of these, lined with tiny, identical, red brick houses, nestling snug against each other. A group of small children was playing in the road; Ellie had to swerve to avoid their ball game. She noticed George among them and waved, but he was too absorbed in his game to see her – or realise that his scarf was trailing behind him and in danger of getting tangled around his legs.

When she got to Jack's house, halfway down

the street, she found it was even smaller than she remembered. She marvelled that they all fit in, especially with Will and Jack grown so big.

After leaning her bicycle against the front wall, Ellie noticed that the door was ajar. Without thinking, she pushed through it and into the small hallway. Light was coming from the kitchen so she strode in, pulling herself up short when she saw Mrs Scott sitting at the kitchen table, staring into the distance, her face stained with tears, twisting a handkerchief round and round in her hands.

Ellie swallowed an exclamation of shock and began to back out of the room, but just then Mrs Scott looked up.

"Ellie! What a lovely surprise! It's been a long time since we've seen you here!" Her voice sounded thick, but she stretched her mouth into a broad smile as though nothing out of the ordinary were happening.

"I know, I'm so sorry, I didn't mean to intrude."

"Not at all, don't be silly!" Mrs Scott wiped her eyes with a studied casual air. "Jack's not home from work yet but he won't be long. Won't you stay for a cup of tea? It's so nice to see you."

"Well, if you really don't mind. . ."

"Of course not." Mabel bustled around the kitchen, filling the kettle and putting it on the range. All the while she kept up a stream of questions; about school, about Ellie's family, about how Thomas was getting on at the surgery. . . She seemed delighted with the mince pies and exclaimed over how delicious they smelled.

It was in the middle of one of these rhapsodies of praise that she was interrupted by a loud snore from the other room. Just like that, Mabel's face crumpled. She turned away quickly, feigning a need to refill the milk jug, but not before Ellie had seen her expression.

"Mrs Scott . . . is . . . is everything all right? Was that . . . Mr Scott?"

"You really must call me Mabel, Ellie. I'm fine, my dear, just fine. Yes, that's Joe." She gave a bright laugh that rang shrilly through the kitchen. "I'm afraid he's had one too many at The Dog and is sleeping it off. He . . . ah . . . he was sent home from the factory today."

Mabel still had her back turned, but there was something so sad in the droop of her shoulders that Ellie felt tears welling in her own eyes.

"Was . . . was that why you were crying?"

"Ah. . ."

Ellie got to her feet and went to stand beside the older woman. After a few seconds, and a little nervously, she put her arm around her. Mabel seemed to collapse under this small gesture, her shoulders shaking.

"Oh, goodness, what a silly fuss," she mumbled. "I am sorry, Ellie."

"Please don't be sorry! But . . . is there anything I can do? I don't like to see you like this."

"Oh, I'm fine, really, quite all right." Mabel shook her head as though to clear it. "So silly, making such a scene, when so many are much worse off."

Ellie led her back to the table and they sat down side by side. Mabel's hand found its way to Ellie's.

"You're not making a scene. But sometimes it helps to talk about things," Ellie suggested cautiously.

Another tear trickled down Mabel's nose. "I . . . I can't really."

"I promise I won't say anything. Is it about Mr Scott? Is he . . . unwell again?" Ellie blushed, unsure how to speak about Joe's drinking. "Is he still upset about the white feather. . . ? Or maybe worried about Will?"

"Oh, yes, all of that." Mabel dropped her voice to a whisper. "I shouldn't say anything, but I can't— It's so hard."

Ellie thought of her own mother breaking down in front of Thomas and gave Mabel's hand a reassuring squeeze.

"I never really understood why my Joe was so against the war," Mabel went on, still in hushed tones. "I mean, heaven knows I don't like the idea of it either and I certainly don't like my boy being out there." She paused to blow her nose and dab at her eyes. "But Joe came in the other night from the pub, talking and talking, and I don't think he really knew what he was saying. . . I'm sure he doesn't remember telling me anything, though he begged me not to tell the children. He said . . . he said he had a brother – a brother I never even knew about – who went away to the Boer War. Teddy, he was called."

Ellie's brow furrowed. How strange it must feel to suddenly learn something so significant about your husband. And she remembered, suddenly, Aunt Frances talking about the Boer Wars and how many men she'd known who went away and didn't come back.

"Teddy was a good bit older than Joe and I think he looked up to him, wanted to be like him, you know?" Ellie thought of Charlie gazing longingly at George; George so keen for Jack's approval. "Joe hated being left behind when Teddy went to war. He wanted to join up himself, just like our Jack does now. But . . . but. . ." She took a juddering breath.

"Teddy didn't come home?" Ellie suggested softly.

"No, he did, he did. But honestly it might have been better if he didn't." Ellie couldn't contain a gasp. "I know, my love, it's a terrible thing to say, but he was blind and had a bullet wound to his leg, which had got infected on the ship home. . . He died only a few days after he got back, in an awful amount of pain and completely horrified by what he'd seen and done. My poor Joe has been haunted by these stories ever since. And I just can't stop thinking about it. My poor Will out there now—" She broke off, hand to her chest.

Ellie felt sick. She didn't know what to say. "No . . . no wonder he doesn't want to go to war."

"I know. . . He says he feels ill with fear at the

thought of going, and at the idea that Will is out there, risking his life. . . And he's ashamed, so ashamed. . . I think that's why the . . . the drinking has got so much worse."

Ellie felt a pang of sympathy for the man she'd judged so harshly.

"Oh, Ellie, please don't say anything to our Jack, will you? I feel I've betrayed Joe as it is. But I needed to talk to someone; it was eating me away!"

"I know the feeling," Ellie said. "And I promise I won't say anything to Jack, or to anyone else."

"Oh, goodness, he must be almost home. What will he think if he catches us like this?"

Mabel hurried to the sink to splash her face and Ellie joined her there. They laughed at each other's puffy eyes and blotchy skin – what else could they do? They were still giggling when Jack and Anna returned, both in festive high spirits.

Ellie stayed for a few games of cards, and the Scotts munched on mince pies, praising how tasty they were, though Jack teased her about them all being different sizes and some a little lopsided.

After an hour, Ellie got up to leave. Her mother

would be home from knitting soon. Jack said he'd see her safely back so she wished the others a happy Christmas and they set off, cycling side by side.

They stopped a few yards from her garden gate.

"Just in case your mam's back already," Jack said, eyes wide in mock fear, which made Ellie giggle again. He reached out his hand and she took it, both of them still sitting on their bicycles in the moonlight, looking at each other in silence.

After a long moment she laughed. "Go on home with you, you daft thing!"

"Oh, that's just charming." Jack grinned as he released her hand and turned his bicycle back towards the village. "When exactly are you off to finishing school, Miss Phillips? The sooner the better, I say!"

She was still smiling as she walked into the house. Even the horrible story she'd heard earlier could not entirely dampen her spirits.

Seventeen

Despite everything that had happened over the course of the year, despite Father not being there, Christmas Day was a cheerful affair. Aunt Frances had a few days' leave and had come to stay. And at Ellie's suggestion, Mother had invited Thomas to join them. He wasn't able to leave the surgery for long enough to go back to his parents' home in Norwich.

Ellie and Aunt Frances had prepared the dinner together and, although food wasn't quite as plentiful as on a normal Christmas Day, Ellie thought they had done a good job. Cooking was a lot more fun with Aunt Frances there, telling stories from her past few months nursing.

One soldier she had treated had suffered concussion

from a nasty blow to the head. When he came round, he suddenly spoke fluent French, despite never, as far as anyone knew, having spoken a word of it before. Another had lost a leg – a story which made Ellie shudder. Aunt Frances dreaded him coming round and having to break the news to him. But although he had cried and clung to her hand when she first told him, by the end of the day he was making jokes about it, and a week later had decided that it might even mean he could go to university as he'd always wanted, rather than managing the family estate. They fell silent at the end of this story. How remarkable some people were, Ellie thought.

Mother had made the table look beautiful, getting out the silverware and even lighting some candles. Thomas poured glasses of the sherry for himself, Aunt Frances and Mother, splashing a drop or two into the bottom of a glass for Ellie. She put a beaker of cordial in front of Charlie, who was eyeing the potatoes greedily. Thomas raised his glass.

"Thank you to the wonderful Phillips ladies for preparing this delicious meal and inviting me to join you. Thank you for making me so welcome in Endstone and helping me to settle in here. Merry Christmas!"

"Merry Christmas!" they all echoed, chinking their glasses together.

Ellie glanced nervously at her mother and took a tiny sip of her sherry. It felt as though she'd swallowed one of the candles as it burned its way down her throat and pooled warmly in her stomach.

"I'd like to raise a toast to Wesley—" Josephine said.

"And all our boys out there," Aunt Frances chipped in. Ellie's mother gave her a look but for once didn't argue.

"Yes, to all our boys out in France. I hope they have a very happy Christmas."

"Hear, hear," the others piped up, tapping their glasses together again.

"Do you think Father got our parcel?" Ellie asked. She and her mother had sent chocolate, magazines and a pair of gloves that Ellie had finally managed to complete.

"I don't know, but we sent it in plenty of time, so I hope so."

They hadn't had a Christmas card from him yet, or indeed any letters since the one telling them he wouldn't be home for Christmas. But now they knew the kind of hold-ups that could occur, they were trying hard not to worry.

"I'm sure Wes will be back with us in plenty of time for next Christmas," Aunt Frances declared and they all agreed heartily. Ellie pushed thoughts of Billie Farrow and of Joe Scott's brother Teddy to the back of her mind.

After dinner they all helped clear the plates away and then played cards by the fire in the living room. After a while, Mother nodded off in her easy chair and Ellie went to make tea for the others. As she passed the kitchen window, she caught sight of something flickering across the pool of light that spilled out into the darkness. She grinned when she recognized the familiar figure astride his bicycle, still wearing the red paper crown from a cracker.

Ellie hurriedly took the pot of tea back through to the living room with cups, milk, sugar and some of her home made mince pies. She was pleased to see that her mother was still dozing. Aunt Frances was cuddling

Charlie on her lap, humming "Away in a Manger". Even Thomas was looking a little drowsy.

Ellie put the tray down on a low table. "It's a bit stuffy in here. I'm just going to get some fresh air. I won't be long."

"Mmm?" Aunt Frances murmured sleepily. "All right then. Ellie?" Ellie turned impatiently from the doorway. "Say happy Christmas to Jack from us."

Ellie gave a sheepish smile. She ran upstairs to grab a small package from under her pillow and to pile on her outdoor clothes, before joining her friend at the front of the house.

Jack had leaned his bicycle against the fence and was standing with his hands in his pockets. Without preamble, he grabbed Ellie's hand and began to tug her away from the house.

"Jack!"

"Shhh! Clifftop!" was all he said.

Further up the hill from Ellie's house, fields gave way to the cliff edge. There was a sheltered spot, just under the overhang of the cliff, which required a bit of scrabbling to get to and which, hidden from the path, no one else seemed to know about. It had been a favourite hiding place for Jack and Ellie when they were younger, though they hadn't visited it as often in recent years.

Wriggling into it now, Ellie knew why; their longer limbs were cramped in the small space. Eventually they settled on a position facing each other, backs against the sides of the nook, knees bent and legs overlapping.

"Perfect!" Jack announced.

"Oh, yes, perfect," Ellie agreed, laughing as she wriggled her feet against the early tinglings of pins and needles.

They looked out over the sea, which looked like molten silver in the moonlight, and were silent for a long moment.

"It is beautiful here," Jack conceded at last. "I'll miss it when I go away."

"*When*. . ." Ellie teased.

"Oh, I'm going, El. We always knew Endstone wasn't big enough for us, didn't we? It's not a bad old place, really, but there's so much more of the world out there. Why should we settle for this?"

Ellie had no answer. It was true.

"I'm not sure how much longer I can stick it at the

factory. It feels so dull and pointless – it's killing me! Especially when there are so many of our boys over in Europe doing something that matters. And not just older boys either."

This was true too. Every week there was another story of a boy lying about his age to join up, and while a lot of them were sent home with a flea in their ear, just as many were getting through. Ellie glanced over at Jack. He could easily be one of the ones who got through. He scarcely looked like a little boy any more – he was for ever being mistaken for older than his years.

It seemed as though the war would be going on for a lot longer than anyone had originally anticipated. Jack might actually be able to go. She repressed a shudder, remembering his uncle Teddy whom he had never known or even known about. But at the same time, there was no denying that joining up would give Jack an opportunity to get out of Endstone that he would never otherwise have had.

"That bored of my company, are you?" she said finally. It was a last-ditch effort and not a card she relished playing, but she wasn't quite ready to give her blessing to his plan.

"Oh, give over!" he laughed, clamping one of her shins between his two and squeezing tight. "Since when do you play the high society lady fishing for compliments?"

Ellie was glad of the darkness so he couldn't see her blushing.

He cleared his throat. "Shall we change the subject?"

"Good idea!" Ellie said gratefully. "Do you want your Christmas present or what?"

"That depends," Jack said seriously. "Did you make it yourself?"

Ellie blushed even more deeply and lashed out at him with her right foot.

"Easy! Are you trying to tip me the cliff and on to those rocks?"

"That depends," Ellie mimicked in acid tones. "What were you saying about your gift?"

"Why, only that I really hoped you'd made it yourself!" said Jack, a picture of wide-eyed innocence. "Now give it here." He reached out and tickled her, and as her hands flew out to swat him away, he quickly dipped his hand into her pocket and tugged out the parcel, wrapped in now-crumpled brown paper. "Ah ha!" He tore off the paper and pulled out a long cornflower blue scarf.

It was different widths along its considerable length and a slightly different shade of blue at the very end where she'd run out of wool, but Ellie was proud of her creation. Or, at least, she had been. Looking at it again now, she felt strangely shy.

"Ah, El, it's mad and beautiful, just like you. I shall treasure it," Jack declared solemnly, as he wrapped it round – and round, and round – his neck. Before she could puzzle this statement out, he had pulled a small package from his own pocket and tossed it into her lap.

"I love the gift-wrapping," Ellie remarked wryly, gesturing towards the layers of newspaper.

"Waste not, want not!" Jack intoned. "Now, hurry up – my bum's going numb!"

Ellie tore off the paper to reveal a large, white cockle shell – the biggest she had ever seen. It filled the palm of her hand completely. "It's lovely. . ." she began.

"Turn it over."

Ellie did so and squinted. Something was painted on the smooth inside of the shell – not a millimetre was left uncovered. Holding it up so that the moonlight fell on it, she gasped. It was a map – a map of the world. There was Europe, the Americas, Africa. . . Ellie ran her finger over it, marvelling at the detail.

Jack was watching her keenly. "You wouldn't believe how many hours I spent in the library, copying that from an atlas. And you know how I feel about that place!"

She looked at the tiny details and found it easy to believe. It was, to borrow one of her father's expressions, a real labour of love. And Ellie knew very well how Jack felt about the library. When they were younger, she would often try to drag him there, especially when they'd had a delivery of new books. They had been thrown out for being noisy more times than she cared to remember, then, to cap it all, he had managed to ruin an expensive book by falling asleep and knocking a pot of ink over it. It had taken him months to earn the money to replace it and, as far as she knew, he'd never been back since.

"I thought, you know, this way you could carry the world around in your pocket. Until you get to visit it yourself, I mean."

She realized that she had not yet spoken. "Jack. . . It's just . . . it's perfect."

He looked pleased, then quickly adopted a smug expression, crossing his arms behind his head. "I thought so. Come on, shall we go? It's freezing out here and your mum will have my guts for garters if she notices you're gone."

"Oh, not yet. Please? Just five more minutes, all right?"

"All right," he agreed, "five more minutes."

They sat watching the moon reflected on the surface of the sea, the dark clouds drifting lazily across the sky and the white wave cap breaking on the rocks below, the only sounds the whispering of the water and wind and the hooting of night birds. And when they finally came to leave, they had lost all feeling in their feet and legs and had to hobble the whole way back to Ellie's house, grasping each other's arms for support.

Ellie's moving story continues...

ELLIE'S WAR

Wherever You Are

EMILY SHARRATT

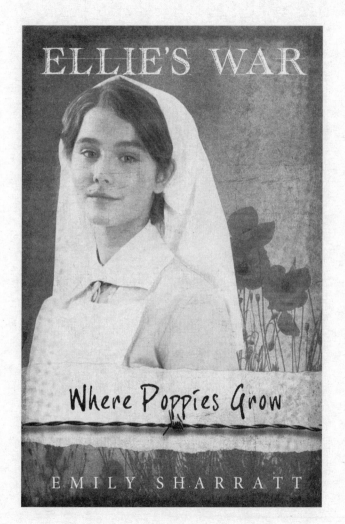

ELLIE'S WAR

Where Poppies Grow

EMILY SHARRATT

ELLIE'S WAR

The Final Ashes

EMILY SHARRATT